MAUI MURDER

Charlotte Gibson Mysteries #2

JASMINE WEBB

Chapter 1

"Give me all your money," the man who had just walked into the ice cream shop demanded. "Come on, quickly."

I sighed. "Seriously, dude?"

"Bitch, I said I want the money from the register."

"First of all, don't call me a bitch. Second, I've been robbed by *way* more intimidating men than you before. Third, you're trying to rob me with a butter knife. Do you really think I'm scared of that?"

The guy in front of me swayed as he tried to process the words I'd just said; he was obviously drunk out of his mind.

Now, I wasn't exactly an idiot. Not most of the time, anyway. If I was truly, legitimately being robbed by someone, I wasn't silly enough to try and play hero. I'd give them all the cash in the register, swear with my friendliest smile that I'd forget what they looked like as soon as they walked out the door, and do whatever it would take to survive. I knew Leslie, my boss, wouldn't have a problem with it. And if she did, well, too bad.

No job was worth my life.

But at the same time, I had standards. And I wasn't going to just hand over a couple hundred bucks to some loser who'd had too much to drink last night and was still under the influence now, at ten in the morning. If you wanted to rob me, you had to put a modicum of effort in.

"I told you to give me the cash," the man shouted, loudly this time.

"No."

"I will stab you with this, you hear me?" He waved the plastic butter knife in front of my face, and I snatched it out of his hand, snapping it in half in front of him. He stared at me for a minute then howled in anger.

"Witch! You're a witch!"

He took a couple steps back then rushed up to the counter and began trying to climb over it. Of course, being drunk and not the fittest guy in the world to begin with, it didn't exactly go the way he had probably hoped. He was stopped by the rounded glass of the ice cream display cabinet and slid back down to the ground.

I pulled out my phone and dialed 911, but before I got a chance to connect with the operator, he began backing up, and I realized he was going to try again but this time with a running start. I pulled a giant fifteen-gallon tub of Cookie Monster ice cream from the display case. It was nearly empty, which was exactly what I wanted.

I put the phone on speaker as I had an idea.

"911, what is your emergency?"

"Hi, I'm working at Aloha Ice Cream on South Kihei Road, and there's a man here who's trying to rob me," I said as the man stared me down.

He shuffled his feet like he was pretending to be a bull about to charge. Well, he could charge all he wanted. I was ready.

"I'm sending police over now. Are you safe, ma'am?"

"I should be okay," I replied. "He's drunk and tried to threaten me with a butter knife. I'm not exactly dealing with Norman Bates over here."

That was when the man charged. He roared as he ran toward the ice cream cabinet as fast as he could, launching himself off one leg to try and jump the whole display case.

Unfortunately for him, he overestimated his capabilities, as so many of us have done in the past while under the influence. He made it about three-quarters of the way over, but his legs caught on the display cabinet, and he plummeted headfirst toward the ground.

This was what I'd been expecting and what I was waiting for. I shoved the tub of ice cream over his head and shoulders even as he was still in the air, and he plummeted to the floor with a crash and a bang.

"What the hell?" he shouted, his voice muffled. "What the hell is this?"

The man scrambled to his feet and tried to get the ice cream container off his head, but because I'd shoved it firmly over his shoulders, his arms were pinned to his sides, and he was incapable of doing it.

Instead, he started shouting and ran directly into the wall, falling fair onto his ass.

"What is the matter with you?" he screamed.

"Ma'am, is everything all right?" the 911 operator asked in a calm voice.

I watched the unfolding scene while biting my lip to stop myself from laughing. This was easily the most hilarious attempted robbery I'd ever seen.

"I believe I've got the robber subdued," I said. "I'm safe right now."

"Good. The police are on their way. Please stay on the line."

"I'm not going anywhere."

The robber, on the other hand, was very much going places. Or attempting to, at least. He struggled to get back to his feet but eventually managed it and began making a beeline for the door.

"You're a crazy person!" he shouted as he tripped over a chair next to one of the three small tables set up by the window. He fell to the ground and rolled a couple of times before hitting the doorframe and coming to a stop. I snickered as he struggled to his feet once more, even wobblier than he had been before. The guy had to be especially dizzy by now. A giant glob of blue Cookie Monster ice cream—it was basically chocolate chip cookie dough with the vanilla ice cream base dyed blue—fell from the container and onto the floor.

He stepped on the ice cream and slipped, barely managing to stay upright as he found the doorway and ran out into the street.

Horns immediately began honking, and tires squealed as the cars on the busy road ahead tried to avoid the crazy dude running into traffic with an ice cream bucket on his head.

"What is wrong with you?" someone shouted from their car window, and I watched with a combination of curiosity and horror as the guy ran onto the beach, still trying to get the bucket off his head.

Eventually, he ran headlong into a tree and must have knocked himself out, because he fell to the ground. A slow leak of blue ice cream began pooling next to him while a crowd of onlookers gathered. Flashing red-and-blue lights in the distance told me the cops were just about here.

My boss, Leslie, chose that moment to show up for the day.

"Hi, Charlie. What's up?"

"We're out of Cookie Monster ice cream," I replied. Leslie looked outside, spotted the gallon bucket on the man's head as the police approached, and raised her eyebrows, like this was a slightly out-of-the-ordinary occurrence and nothing more. I had to hand it to her; Leslie was cool as a cucumber.

"You sure do have a knack for attracting strange characters."

"Tell me about it."

THANKFULLY, THE REST OF THE DAY PASSED BY relatively uneventfully. Well, after I'd explained the whole story to the police and they'd taken the man to the station to sleep it off before he was arrested for attempted robbery. I was hoping for a pretty easy day. After all, I was meeting my best friend, Zoe, at four to look at an apartment the two of us were considering renting.

After Zoe had been stalked and attacked by a creep in her apartment, she'd been staying with Mom and me. She still hadn't been able to bring herself to stay in the apartment, and we ended up finding the perfect solution: Zoe would rent out her apartment to cover her costs, while she and I would split a two-bedroom place. It was perfect. A two-bedroom was usually less than double the price of a one bedroom, which fit my budget a little bit better, and now that I had the hundred grand I'd earned for solving James MacMahon's murder a month ago, I was better situated to pay rent.

On top of that, Zoe's job as a doctor looked amazing on rental application forms. Much better than ice cream server and occasional robbery foiler.

"You'll have to make sure you don't get scammed," Leslie said to me during a lull in the middle of the day. "There's a lot of frauds out there."

"Agreed," I said. "So many scammers on Craigslist. People who claim they're stuck on the mainland or overseas for some reason, and so they'll have to mail the keys, but first you have to pay the deposit by money order. Right."

"Exactly," Leslie said, shaking her head. "It's incredible how many people out there think it's acceptable to try and rip off others."

"They usually take the photos on the ad from Airbnb listings," I said.

"That would be easy."

"And then, of course, there's the creeps."

"Yes, you have to watch out for that."

"Well, on the bright side, some of them out themselves as perverts before you even email them."

"Really? They're not subtle?"

I laughed and pulled up a screenshot I'd taken of a Craigslist ad. I was actually considering starting a Facebook group titled "creepy Craigslist apartment listings," but I didn't have the follow-through to actually keep it going.

I passed the phone to Leslie so she could read the advertisement, and her expression went from slightly skeptical to purely horrified right in front of me.

I grinned as she handed me back the phone. "I think I just lost a bit of faith in humanity."

Glancing down, I reread the ad.

Wanted: female roommate. This is a great deal for the perfect woman. Rent is a very discounted $400 a month for your own private room, as long as you are willing to follow these rules:

- *When in all common areas, you must be willing to wear a penguin suit, provided by me.*

- *When wearing the penguin suit, you will only quack like a penguin*
- *If I'm home and you're in the suit, you must only eat fish. Don't worry, I work almost every night, so most of the time you'll be free to eat other things. Or, you're welcome to cook whatever you want and eat it in your room in private.*
- *You must at all times do your best to act like you are a real penguin. I have received numerous applications from women who weren't serious about truly becoming a penguin while living in this home.*
- *Obviously your room is your private space, and I don't care at all what you do in there.*

There is no requirement for sex. I'm not some weirdo.

I snickered as my eyes scanned over it once more, and Leslie shook her head. "That guy is *definitely* sexually attracted to penguins."

"You got that right. But he says it right there in the ad: he's not some kind of weirdo."

Leslie laughed. "Well, if he's written it in the ad, it must be true. Seriously, this is the sort of thing you have to deal with these days?"

"At least this guy was up front with his penguin fetish," I said. "Some of them are more of a surprise to be discovered after you've signed a year-long lease."

Leslie shook her head. "Well, I hope the place you and Zoe have lined up to look at doesn't come with any weird roommates."

"Not to worry about that. We're getting a place to ourselves."

"Good. And obviously, if you need a reference, feel free to get them to call me. I'll tell anyone who asks that you're the assistant manager here."

"Aww, thank you," I said. "I appreciate it."

"Not a problem. It's hard for your generation out there. I get it."

There were some downsides to working at Aloha Ice Cream, and I certainly didn't plan on it being a permanent career, but I had had far worse bosses than Leslie in my time on this earth.

Chapter 2

Zoe picked me up after work and immediately began driving north on South Kihei Road to get us to our viewing appointment.

"This place should be good," she said. "It belongs to the mother of one of the nurses at the hospital. She wants someone responsible to rent it. And she's willing to give us a discount on it, because her daughter knows me and says we'll be good tenants. Two grand a month."

"A grand each? I can handle that," I said.

"Exactly. It's an amazing deal, so I'm really hoping this works out."

Zoe pulled up in front of a building that looked relatively modern, probably built in the late nineties or early two thousands. It was low-rise, with a rendered brick exterior and plain but neat landscaping. We parked in the visitor's spot at the back and waited for the nurse's mom to show up.

"So, how's the ice cream shop going?" Zoe asked.

"It can't be nearly as exciting as trying to find a killer, but it's a much safer job."

"I don't know about that; a guy tried to rob me today."

Zoe's mouth dropped open. "You're joking."

I recounted the entire story, and by the time I finished, Zoe was laughing so hard tears streamed down her cheeks.

"You are insane. Completely insane. You do realize you could have just given him the money in the cash register, right?" Zoe asked.

"I mean, yeah. But the guy was plastered, he had no weapon at all, and he seemed to genuinely believe he could leap over the entire display cabinet in a single bound. I wasn't about to let a guy like that just take some cash because he asked for it."

Zoe rolled her eyes. "You're ridiculous, you know that?"

"What? If some guy came into the hospital half falling over, would you give him all the morphine he wanted?"

"No, of course not. That would be insane."

"Then why would you expect me to do the same? The guy was clearly not going to be able to overpower me. Trust me, I know when to just hand over the cash, and this wasn't it. As evidenced by the fact that he knocked himself out running into a tree."

"He's lucky he didn't get run over by the sounds of it."

"Yeah. I think the cop who interviewed me wanted to mention that then thought better of it."

"Oh, there's Val's mom," Zoe said suddenly, getting out of the car and waving to a woman who looked to be in her early sixties. Obviously active and very spry for her age, slim, with short gray hair and blue eyes that glimmered in the sun, Val's mother jogged over toward us.

"You must be Zoe and Charlotte," the woman said. She wiped her palms on her shirt then shook Zoe's hand as I got out of the car and came around to do the same with me. "I'm Iris."

"Call me Charlie. It's nice to meet you," I said to her with a smile.

"And you. Come on in. Let's go take a look at this apartment."

Iris led us through the secure front door of the building, and we took the stairs up to the second floor. "This apartment is really well located," Iris told us as we walked down the hallway. It was clean, bright, and well maintained, all of which boded well for the property. "I bought it about twenty years ago, and I planned on retiring in it, but in the end, I decided to travel quite a bit more than I was expecting, and I can't justify holding onto a two-bedroom when I'm in town for two months of the year. My last tenant was here for eight years, but she recently moved to the mainland for a new job, so it's back on the market. Here you go, ladies."

Iris opened the door to apartment number 27, and Zoe and I followed her inside. It was clean and bright, and while the square footage wasn't enormous, high ceilings made it feel bigger than it was. The floors were hardwood, the paint new, the kitchen modern and updated. I immediately liked it.

Making my way through the living room, I headed over to the lanai. It offered up a great view of the inland mountains, and a warm breeze wafted over. Yes, this would be the perfect place to spend a relaxing morning with a newspaper and coffee.

"I hear you have a dog. Is that right?" Iris asked me when I walked back in, and I nodded.

"Yeah. Coco is tiny, she's a dachshund mix, and she's very well behaved."

"Oh, I'm sure she is," Iris said. "You're welcome to have a pet here. After all, pets are family."

"Great," I said, a wave of relief washing over me. I knew from experience that finding a place to rent that was pet friendly was often quite the ordeal.

Zoe and I looked through the bedrooms, and I had to say, I was really pleased.

"Well, I won't pressure you two into saying yes right away," Iris told us when we'd finished looking. "Zoe has my number. Just let me know. If you two want to sign a lease, Val says you're responsible, so I trust you."

"Thank you so much," I said.

We left the apartment and got back into the car. Zoe put it into gear and turned to me.

"So what do you think?"

"I think we've found a new place to live."

Zoe grinned. "I'm glad you think so. I love it too. I'll let Iris know tomorrow that we're willing to sign a lease."

I leaned back against the seat and sighed. "Wonderful. This place is so amazing. I'm going to get to move out. I'm pretty sure if Mom tells me one more time that men don't like women who solve murders, there's going to be another body out there."

Zoe laughed. "She should love your story from today."

"No kidding. Seriously though, I'm glad we're getting a place together. I promise you won't hate me after a week," I said with a wink.

"Same here. Anyway, I'm just going to drop you off at home and then go to work. I'm on the night shift again this week."

"And it's a full moon too."

"Tell me about it," Zoe muttered. "I know studies have been done, and I know science doesn't back up the idea that all the crazy stuff happens at the full moon, but anyone who's worked an emergency department knows it's a real thing."

"Well, good luck. Try not to get stabbed by a crazy person."

"I'll do my best," Zoe said with a smile.

Ten minutes later she pulled up in front of my mom's house. I got out of the car, waved a quick goodbye to my friend, and headed inside.

"So, how was the apartment?" Mom asked as I headed into the kitchen and grabbed a beer out of the fridge.

"Great! It's really nice, and the price is right for both of us."

"I'm glad to hear it. Although I do wish you had

picked somewhere with a little bit more privacy. How are you supposed to bring a man home when you have a roommate?"

I rolled my eyes. "Easy. I'm not bringing any home."

Mom shook her head. "How do you ever intend to get married and have children if you don't have any boyfriends? Are you a lesbian? It's all right if you are."

I almost spat out my beer. "What? No, I'm straight, Mom. If I was gay, I would tell you. I'm just not interested in a relationship right now. And if I am, I can sort it out with Zoe, who is also an adult woman, and one I would much rather have this conversation with than you. No offense. I promise, it'll be fine."

"You're not getting any younger, you know," Mom said, giving me a hard look.

"And you're not going to get any older if you keep up this conversation," I replied in the fakest perky voice I could manage.

"Ha ha, very funny, Charlie," Mom said. "Well, as long as you're happy with the place, I'm happy for you both. What would you like as a housewarming gift?"

I shrugged. "I guess I didn't really expect anything."

"Well, I'll surprise you. I can't let my daughter move into her own place here on the island and not get her anything."

"All right, thanks, Mom," I said, giving her a quick hug. "I love you."

"I love you too, Charlie. I'm proud of you, you know."

Warmth flooded my cheeks. My mom could be annoying, but I knew she loved me. "Thanks."

I finished the beer then decided to take Coco out for a walk along the beach. After all, it was a beautiful early-November night in Maui, and even though the sun had gone down a few hours ago, it was still around seventy degrees out.

As soon as I grabbed Coco's leash, she began jumping around my feet, and as soon as we left, she strained on the leash, immediately heading for the beach. As it had turned out, it was Coco's favorite place. She wasn't a big fan of the water—when you're about eight inches tall, it doesn't take too big an errant wave to ruin your day—but she loved running along the sand, chasing sticks, and sniffing everything she could.

When Coco came home with her little belly covered in sand, you could be sure she'd had a fun walk.

"All right, all right, I'm coming," I said with a laugh as I stepped up the pace to a kind of half-jog as Coco strained like crazy against the leash while she walked down the sidewalk. We reached the southern end of Waipuilani Park, and we crossed through the expanse of grass and straight to the beach. It was low tide, so there was plenty of sand for Coco to run through, but my attention was immediately caught by something happening at the other end of the park.

Something was going on past the tennis courts. Strong lights shone down on the ground, and a large crowd gathered near the cluster of palm trees a little ways away. Maybe a movie filming a nighttime beach scene?

"Come on, Coco," I said. "Let's go check it out." After all, if it *was* a movie, you never knew who was in it. Hawaii was great for attracting talent. When *Hawaii Five-0* was still on the air, it regularly got incredible guest stars, because as it turned out that "Hey, want to come hang out in tropical paradise and get paid for a few days' worth of work?" was a great way to lure A-list talent.

"I'm hoping for Matt Damon," I said to Coco. "They should have filmed *The Martian* here. After all, don't you think Hawaii looks more like Mars than the Jordanian desert?"

Coco shot me a look that said she thought I was a total idiot. Fair enough.

As we got closer to the shoot, however—we were delayed by Coco needing to sniff every grain of sand on the way—I began to realize this wasn't a movie after all. Yellow police tape cordoned off a large part of the beach, and a dark van in the nearby parking lot had "Maui County Coroner's Office" printed on it in white block letters.

My heart sank. Another death on the water. Kanaloa, the Hawaiian god of the ocean, had struck again. I had always been an indoor kid. Sure, I liked hanging out on the beach and getting a tan, but actually going in the water? No thank you. That was Zoe's territory or my dad's. And Dad had always instilled in me a healthy respect for the ocean.

"It's an environment we don't naturally belong in. We can visit, but we have to be careful."

Unfortunately, a lot of people who came to the island didn't understand the true power and force the ocean possessed. And it looked as though it had claimed another victim.

I sighed, sending up a silent prayer for the person who had lost their life, and was about to turn around and continue walking Coco. After all, I wasn't about to stand around, hoping for a glance at the body. And that was when my eyes locked with Jake's.

Jake Llewelyn was one of the hottest but also one of the most frustrating men I'd ever known. He had dark hair that had that constant just-got-out-of-bed look and blue eyes that contrasted beautifully with that hair. It should have been illegal to be as good looking as he was.

It was too bad he was a cop whose partner had Tased me, and while he seemed to genuinely care about crime on Maui, he could be ridiculously pigheaded, especially when it came to following the law in situations that the law couldn't necessarily cover.

That was basically my way of saying he got annoyed whenever I involved myself in police matters, even if my involvement actually prevented a worse crime.

I turned to leave, resisting the urge to say hi to him. But before I got the chance, Jake strode over toward me, motioning for me to follow him to the end of the police tape, where we could speak away from anyone else.

"What are you doing here?" he asked when we had finally moved away, his blue eyes boring into mine.

I shrugged. "Walking Coco. I didn't realize that was illegal now."

Jake's eyes flashed, but I couldn't quite make out what it meant. Anger? Frustration? Something else?

"It's not illegal. I just don't trust you."

"Trust me about what? Someone drowned on the beach. What could I possibly have had to do with it?" Then realization hit me, and my eyes widened. "Oh. They didn't drown."

Jake pursed his lips, obviously annoyed at himself for having let slip enough that I figured it out. "I can't talk to you about an open investigation."

"Another murder on the island, hey? That's two in a few weeks. Pretty rare around these parts."

"Yeah. That's about the quota for the year filled up. Some years are crazier than others."

"I guess so. Well, I hope you find who did it. Try to stop your partner from Tasering any innocent people."

Jake narrowed his eyes at me. "You're eventually going to have to let that one go."

"Am I, though?"

"This was a mistake. Anyway, I assume I don't have to tell you to stay out of this investigation?"

"So long as no one is offering an extra hundred grand for solving it."

"You're impossible."

"You're the one who dragged me over here to chat."

"And I always seem to regret it. Now, if you'll excuse me, I have to get back to my case."

I shook my head as Jake walked off. Why had he called me over here anyway if he thought I was so hard to deal with? It wasn't as if he could have expected me to want in on the case. Men were impossible to figure out sometimes.

No, not sometimes. All the time.

Turning around, I moved past the crowd and headed back the way I came with Coco. Hopefully, Jake would solve the case. I had no intention of getting myself involved.

Chapter 3

I woke up the next morning and took Coco for another quick walk along the beach—this time avoiding the spot where the person had been killed the night before. Had they been murdered on the beach itself? Or had they been dumped from a boat and floated to shore?

Even if I didn't plan on actually getting involved in the case, I still wondered. After all, I was a fan of *My Favorite Murder*, a podcast featuring true-crime stories. And here I was, with yet another true crime in my own backyard. It was only natural that I would have questions.

Letting Coco back in the house, I took Mom's car and drove to work. I was going to have to get something of my own soon. After all, it would be hard to steal Mom's car to get to work if I wasn't living in her house anymore.

The idea of having my own place again lifted my spirits, and once I'd parked and walked along to Aloha

Ice Cream, I browsed Craigslist, checking out the used-car market. After all, I might have had a decent windfall come in, but I wasn't a *total* idiot when it came to money. I wanted to make it last, and I wasn't about to go blow it all on a brand-new BMW. All I needed was something that would get me from point A to point B without exploding.

And okay, sure. I wanted something a little bit sexier than a Honda Accord. So sue me. I was immediately drawn to a 2017 Dodge Challenger RT. I could pretend I was from *Magnum P.I.* or something with that car. But of course, it was thirty grand, and I put the idea out of my head. I wanted to spend five grand, tops.

It was a sexy car, though…

"How was the place?" Leslie asked when I walked through the door.

"Great," I replied with a grin. "We're taking it."

"Congratulations. It's nice to see you putting down some more permanent roots on the island."

I nodded. "Yeah, it is. I didn't want to come back, really. And I had planned on it being a short-term thing. But the more time I spend here, the more I like it."

"The island tends to have that effect on people," Leslie said with a wink.

I smiled. There were a lot of good memories here. But there was also a lot of pain. My father had died when I was sixteen, and Dad had loved the island. I'd sworn I'd never come back, and while I was happy here, every time I saw someone surfing, or saw a

Hawaiian petrel—his favorite bird—flying overhead, a pang of pain hit me in the chest.

"Well, not everyone's having a good time," I said. "Someone was murdered again yesterday. The cops were at the beach last night while I was walking Coco."

"I heard," Leslie said, shaking her head. "She was a local too."

"No kidding. Who was it?"

"Jo Lismore," Leslie said. "My daughter Sam went to school with her. She's probably about five years younger than you. Her family is fairly rich but very down-to-earth. I didn't know Jo well, but she always seemed very nice to me."

"The name seems kind of familiar, but I don't think I knew her," I said.

"It's sad, really. Sam didn't know her well either, but I remember her as a little girl with pigtails who spent an entire birthday party collecting shells on the beach," Leslie said with a small smile. "It must have been her fifth or sixth birthday. Everyone else was playing together, and the birthday girl was perfectly content walking by herself, looking for cool-looking shells. Her mother shrugged when I brought it up and said as long as Jo was happy, that was the important thing. That's how I'll always remember her. I can't believe she was murdered."

"I'm sorry," I said to Leslie.

"Well, I didn't really know her. I only saw her a handful of times. Still, it's quite sad. I gave Sam the day off today. Luckily, we have a few days' worth of ice cream in the freezer, and I can always pop on back there and make it myself if we need to."

"That was really good of you."

Leslie shrugged. "It's what any mother—or good boss—would do."

Our first customer of the day chose that moment to enter, and our conversation was interrupted while we set about serving tourists and locals delicious ice cream. It was a hot day today, especially given the time of year, and we were busy. I was just thrilled to be in an air-conditioned store, occasionally able to lean into the freezing cabinet containing the ice cream.

Frankly, as far as minimum wage jobs went on the island, this one was pretty good. It sure beat being outside when the temperature was in the nineties and humid, anyway.

Around lunchtime, a man walked in. His eyes were red rimmed, betraying the fact that he'd recently been crying, and his lips were pressed together hard, as if he was going through some horrible pain.

"Can I help you?" I asked tentatively, but Leslie gasped when she saw him.

"Randall," she said. "Oh, Randall, I'm so sorry."

Confused, I took a step back and let Leslie take over.

"Thank you, Leslie. It's been… it's been a rough day. Listen, can I speak to Charlotte? I was told she works here." He looked over at me, question marks in his eyes.

"I'm Charlotte," I said slowly. "Charlie."

"What do you want to speak with her about?"

Leslie asked, voicing the exact sentiment I felt. "Sorry. Yes, of course. Go ahead. Take your time."

Leslie shot me a questioning look, and I replied with a slight shrug of my shoulders as I followed Randall out of the store and into the street. I'd never seen this guy before in my life.

He turned to face me as soon as we were outside. "My name is Randall Lismore," he said by way of introduction, and I let out a barely audible gasp. He nodded. "I guess you've heard, then. My daughter was murdered yesterday."

"I'm so sorry," I told him, my heart immediately going out to the man standing in front of me. I knew what it was like to lose a father. I couldn't begin to imagine what it must be like for a father to lose his daughter.

"Thanks. It's… it's not even quite sunk in yet, I don't think. But it will. And then it will hurt even more. Anyway, I needed to speak with you."

"Forgive me for asking, but why? I didn't know your daughter."

"No, but people tell me you're the woman who solved the murder of James MacMahon a few weeks ago."

"Oh. Yes, that was me."

"Listen, I've spoken to the police detectives working this case. One of them seems competent, but the senior one… well, let's just say I don't feel as though my daughter's killer is going to be found in a reasonable amount of time with him working the case. I want her killer found. I want justice for my little girl, and I'm willing to pay for it. If you're willing to find the killer for me, I'll pay you a hundred grand. Same as that other man's family offered. Plus expenses."

"You're joking, right?" were the words that came out of my mouth.

"I'm serious. You obviously know how to find a killer. I don't care how you do it. I just want you to make sure you find who did this, and with enough evidence to bring them to justice. You do that, the hundred grand is yours. And I'll pay expenses no matter what, even if you don't find the killer."

Wow. This was not at all what I'd been expecting. He wanted me to hunt down a killer? And he was going to pay me for it?

"Sure," I found myself saying. "I'll do it."

I mean, what could go wrong? Sure, the last time I went hunting down a killer for money, I'd almost been killed, but now I was not only a hundred grand richer, but someone else was offering me even *more* money to find another killer?

I wasn't about to say no to that.

Randall's shoulders visibly relaxed as soon as I said yes. "You will?"

I nodded. "Yes."

"Great. Great, that's wonderful news. Thank you. My wife will be relieved. Is there anything you need from me immediately?"

"Your contact details," I said. "I know it's going to be difficult, but I'm going to have to speak with you and your family about Jo, preferably sooner rather than later."

"Of course." Randall pulled out a business card and scribbled a number on it. "Here's my card with all my details and my personal cell phone number. Can I get yours as well? I suspect I'm going to have to screen my calls soon. There will be a lot of attention on this case."

I put my number into his phone. "All right. I'll be in touch. And, um, I'm sorry again."

"Thank you," Randall said. "I appreciate it."

I headed back into the ice cream store, slipping Randall's card into my pocket. My heart felt heavy for the man's grief, and I briefly asked myself if I was doing the right thing.

Of course I was. Randall had come to me, not the other way around. It wasn't as if I had gone to a grieving family and asked for a hundred grand to find the killer. Besides, I was going to get paid even if I didn't succeed. I was actually helping him by doing what he wanted. So the feelings of guilt were quickly pushed aside, and instead, I decided I was going to do what Randall wanted: I was going to find his daughter's killer.

"What did Randall want, if you don't mind me asking?" Leslie asked when I reentered the store and we finally had a moment without any customers.

"He wants to pay me to find Jo's killer," I explained. "He found out I was the person who claimed the reward when James MacMahon was killed, and he doesn't trust the cops on the case. Especially not Liam. He has good instincts. Liam is awful."

My view of the man was only slightly tainted by the whole incident with the Taser.

"Wow," Leslie replied. "Are you going to do it?"

I nodded. "I am."

"Are you sure that's wise? I mean, I know the last time, you solved the crime, but you were also kidnapped and almost murdered yourself by the killer."

"So this time I know what to look out for," I replied. "No more breaking bread with killers to try and get them to admit to what they've done."

"All right," Leslie said, but she didn't sound convinced.

"Don't worry. This will be my side hustle. It won't interfere with my job here at all."

"Most people who decide they need a side hustle make earrings to put on Etsy," Leslie pointed out.

"I was never very good at arts and crafts. Snooping on people, though   that's a whole other story."

"Well, please do stay safe. Do you know how hard it is to find good employees these days?" Leslie asked me with a grin, and I laughed. She was the best boss I could ask for.

Chapter 4

"So, what can you tell me about Jo and her family?" I asked Leslie after the morning rush. I was busy scooping chocolate chip cookie dough ice cream into a stainless steel malt cup, making myself a milkshake for lunch. It was safe to say that working at Aloha Ice Cream had not improved the nutritional quality of my diet, but it sure had improved the taste of my meals.

"They lived in Wailea originally but then came to Kihei when Jo was just a few years old. She and Sam went to the same preschool. They're very well off; he got rich during the dot-com bubble and sold everything before it all collapsed. He's put some of that money into a new software company. I don't know the details of it."

"But basically the short of it is that they're completely loaded."

"Yes. Totally. That said, they were always a down-to-earth family. Eventually, Sam and Jo stopped being in all the same classes, and we drifted apart, but they were always friendly, always polite. They weren't the kinds of people to rub the fact that they had money in anyone's face."

I nodded. That was certainly the impression I'd gotten from Randall. He hadn't flashed a Rolex around, and he'd just been dressed in a polo and slacks. And sure, he was a recently grieving father. I wasn't expecting him to be dressed in his Sunday best. But he seemed approachable and kind, even in the midst of unimaginable pain.

"So you haven't spoken to any of them in a while?"

"Not really, no. Certainly not in three or four years. I wish I could be more helpful."

"It's fine. I'm sure I'll run into others who know them sooner rather than later."

"Oh, you will."

Little did I know I was going to run into that first person and my first suspect—just a little while later.

We were ten minutes away from closing when a guy came in wearing loose surfer shorts, flip-flops, a pair of Oakleys, and nothing else. In his early, maybe mid-twenties, he had a model's body, complete with a tan and a six-pack, and it didn't take long for me to realize he had an insanely obnoxious personality to go with it.

"Yo, hottie, what's up?" he said, giving me a nod before openly checking me out. "Wanna bust outta this joint and let me turn your outie into an innie?"

I was so disgusted it took a second before the look

of horror on my face dissipated long enough for me to reply.

"Well, aren't you just a raging success story of the school system? I'm just curious: did you fail sex ed, or did sex ed fail you?" Seriously? Turn my outie into an innie? I didn't even know what he meant by that, and I wasn't about to find out. I had a couple of guesses, but that was a hard no from me.

"Babe, I've never failed anything when it comes to sex," he said, lowering his sunglasses and looking up at me through them while I fought the urge to throw up.

"Okay, just so we're *abundantly* clear: my vagina has currently crawled up into my uterus, locked itself in, and has a shotgun. So why don't you just order some ice cream and get out of here before you embarrass yourself even more than you already have?"

"Why you gotta be such a buzzkill? I'm celebrating. My ex was killed last night, so now it's time to find a new bun to slip my hot dog into."

"You know, there's a lot to unpack in that sentence, and I think it's probably easier to throw out the whole suitcase, but I have to ask—your ex was killed? You were dating Jo Lismore?"

"Yeah, I was. She had a pair of honkers on her like you wouldn't believe."

Honkers? *Really?*

"Someone finally killed that bitch last night. Serves her right."

"Let me guess, she broke up with you, for reasons I can't *possibly* fathom. Was it that you just know too much about a woman's body?" I shouldn't have been antagonizing this guy. After all, I had been hired to find out who killed Jo, and at this point, I was really hoping it was her ex.

Hell, I'd throw this guy in jail for free.

"She just couldn't handle all of this," the guy said, motioning to his torso while biting his lower lip.

"Yeah, I'm sure that's the reason she gave you when she dumped you. Seriously, what was it?"

"Some bull about how immature I was. How I wasn't a real man, and she wanted someone who could take care of her. Well, you know what? That's crap. I could totally take care of her. Just because my family isn't loaded like hers, she thought she was better than me. Well, she wasn't. Her eyes were spaced funny, and just because her tits were like grapefruits didn't make up for the fact she had an ass I like to call the IHOP special."

Ugh. Just when I started to think this guy couldn't get even more disgusting, he lowered that bar even further.

"So what, did you get mad about it and dump her into the ocean?"

"What are you, some kind of cop?"

"No, I'm asking the obvious question, moron. She dumped you and showed up dead a few days later. I've already figured out you have the IQ of a potato, but surely even you can figure out you're going to be one of the main suspects."

"Aw, what the hell?" the guy replied. He obviously hadn't considered it at all. That was probably why he'd come in here celebrating the fact that his ex had been killed. "Tommy G doesn't murder chicks. He moves on, like a real baller. Plenty of fish in the sea to bang, if you get my drift."

Yeah, that was exactly the impression I got when I looked at this guy. Baller. Not a western version of a *Jersey Shore* wannabe.

"Ew, you're sexually attracted to fish?" I said, loudly enough for the other customers in the store to hear, leading to a few dirty looks being given to Tommy. He opened his mouth a couple of times, obviously not knowing how to reply to me, so I continued. "Listen, where were you last night? Because yeah, you are a suspect in Jo's death, and I've been hired to find her killer. So either you can give me a straight answer, or I can just assume you did it, turn your life upside down, and then hand you over to the cops, who I guarantee will make your life an even bigger hell than I can."

Tommy scoffed. "Who would have hired you to look into her murder? You obviously don't know anything."

I pulled out the card Randall Lismore had given me, showing him who had done it, and Tommy's douche levels dropped about twenty percent.

"Fine. So let's assume you're telling the truth and the old man hired you to find his daughter's murderer. I don't have a clue why he'd do it, but whatever. Tommy's no killer. I was at home last night. When did it happen?"

I shrugged. "I'm not sure. You were home all night?"

"Yeah, I was."

"Doing what?"

Tommy shrugged. "You know. Just hangin'. Playing *Fortnite* with the boys. That sort of thing."

"Can anyone vouch for you?"

"Sure. I have a roommate."

"All right, who is it? I need contact information."

"Jordan Butler. You got a pen and paper or something?"

I grabbed a scrap of paper from the receipt dispenser and handed Tommy a pen, and he scribbled down a phone number for me.

"Here. Now you got me all worried. You're ruining my celebration. This is supposed to be a good day."

I rolled my eyes. "Fine. What flavor of ice cream do you want to celebrate the fact that a fellow human just had their life taken away by someone on this island? Not that you're acting like much of a human being here today."

Tommy scowled at me. "Well, when you put it that way, you make it sound like I shouldn't be thrilled my ex washed up on the beach."

"Wow, imagine that," I deadpanned.

"Whatever. Give me a double-scoop cone of triple chocolate."

I made the cone for Tommy, making sure his scoops were a little bit smaller than I would normally make—I could be petty if I wanted to—before handing it over to him and taking his cash.

"Now, if you change your mind about a good time

later, here's my number," Tommy said with a wink, taking a suggestive lick of his ice cream cone.

"What is it about the interaction we've just had that could *possibly* make you think that's on the table?" Still, I took the card with his phone number on it.

After all, he was still one of my suspects until his alibi checked out. And *boy*, did I ever hope he was the killer.

"The ladies pretend they hate me, but I know they just can't resist all of this. You know, if you're really trying to find the killer, you've got your work cut out for you," Tommy said with a grin. "She was a piece of work, Jo. She really was."

"What do you mean by that?"

"I mean she had some fingers in a few pies her parents wouldn't have approved of," he added with a wink.

"Care to elaborate?"

"Hey, you're the one who's supposedly the detective. I'm not going to make your job too easy for you."

And with that, Tommy left the ice cream shop, leaving me wondering what he was talking about. Was he just an angry ex trying to smear Jo's name, or did he actually know about something illicit Jo had been involved in? Or was he just trying to steer me in the other direction, and he was the real killer? It would have taken a complete moron to openly celebrate the death of the person he had killed, but Tommy wasn't exactly a member of Mensa. I decided to keep my eyes and ears open and see what my investigation uncovered.

I closed up the ice cream shop and pulled out Randall's card. I gave him a call and set up a meeting with him and his wife for that night at six. That would give me some time to go home and present myself a little bit more like a private investigator.

After all, that was what I was now, right? At least as a side gig.

I *really* needed to get my own car.

I DROVE BACK HOME AND TOOK COCO BACK DOWN to the beach, letting her run through the sand, her little legs sinking into the sun-warmed beach as she sprinted along, back and forth, occasionally heading toward the water but never too close.

I browsed Craigslist as I walked, and then I found it. The perfect car.

It was a 1993 Jeep Wrangler. Custom painted neon blue with black hood, doors, and trim. The rims were painted the same blue as the rest of the car, which was striking next to the black tires. It came with a removable canopy, and the ad detailed a ton of work that had been done on it.

She had just under two hundred thousand miles on her and a stick shift. I fell in love instantly.

She was beautiful. She was perfect. She was also over budget.

"Come on. Nine grand for a car that's basically as old as I am?" I muttered to myself as Coco ran over, having found a good doxie-sized stick. I took it from her, playing a bit of tug-of-war before she let it go, and hurled it as far as I could down the beach.

She sprinted after it, her little legs moving as fast as they could, while I sent an email to the owner offering five grand. I had to have that car, but I had to have it at a price that I could justify.

Or so I told myself.

"You look like your name should be Blue Lightning," I said to the ad. Great. I was already naming the car. I really hoped I got a reply from my email saying that it was still available.

Taking Coco home, I tried to put the car out of my mind—after all, I would buy a boring Civic or whatever if I really had to—and focused on my meeting with Jo Lismore's family.

Chapter 5

I hadn't brought anything that could be remotely considered business attire to Hawaii. Hell, I owned exactly one pair of pants, a blouse, and a blazer that I had worn to interviews back in Seattle. The blazer was scratchy and uncomfortable, but I had bought it for fifteen bucks on a clearance rack at the mall, and it did the job.

Luckily, Maui wasn't exactly the sort of place where one had to stick to mainland clothing rules. Here, comfort was more important than looking like you just walked off Wall Street, so I slipped on a pair of dark-blue jeans without any holes in them and a plain, light blue T-shirt. It was basically the island version of business casual.

"Mom, I need the car again," I called out.

"Keys are on the table," she shouted back from the kitchen. "Have you eaten yet?"

"No. Can you save me something?"

"You know, when you're living on your own, you're going to have to fend for yourself, food-wise."

"Fine, don't worry about it. I'll have a bowl of Fruit Loops when I get back."

A sigh came from the kitchen. "That's not a proper dinner. I'm making chicken alfredo. I'll put some in a Tupperware for you; it'll be in the fridge when you get back."

"Thanks, Mom. You're the best."

I swiped the keys off the side table next to the door and headed out into the night. Even though it was early November, there was no need for a jacket. I turned on my phone's GPS app, tossed the phone onto the seat, and let the soothing voice tell me where to go.

The Lismore house was at the south end of Makena Road, past all of the fancy hotels and resorts in Wailea, and it was no less impressive than they were. I drove up a circular drive to a single-story, Asian-style house. Parking the car near the front and hoping that was fine, I crossed over a little wooden bridge that passed over a built-in stream. The architecture made me think of Japan, with clean lines everywhere. The front door was mahogany, with a life-sized Buddha statue on either side of it, along with a number of reed plants.

I knocked cautiously on the door, half expecting a butler in a three-piece suit to answer, but instead, it was Randall who opened the door. He wore the same clothes as he had that morning, but his face was lined more deeply than the last time I'd seen him, and it even looked as if the gray hairs around his temples had become more defined.

"Thank you for coming, Charlie. Please, come on in."

Randall opened the door wide, and I entered to find myself in a beautiful entryway. Exposed mahogany beams contrasted with marble floors and cream-colored walls. An enormous Ming Dynasty vase stood against the far side; it was probably worth more than everything I owned combined. Randall led me down a hallway and past a dining room that opened onto the world's largest lanai, followed by an enormous half-moon pool that looked over the Pacific Ocean.

We passed into an enormous living room. A wood accent wall with tiled squares drew the eye toward the two cream-colored couches in front of it, with a live-edge acacia coffee table between them. A fan with leaf-shaped blades slowly spun above, but it was the person sitting on the sofa who drew most of my attention.

This had to be Jo Lismore's mother. The woman's frame was tiny, made even smaller by the way she was partially hunched over on the sofa. Her blond hair reached just past her shoulders and covered her face as she cried softly into a tissue. My heart broke for the poor woman; I couldn't imagine what she was going through.

"Heather," Randall said, his voice a little bit hoarse, "this is Charlotte. The woman I've hired to find Jo's…"

He trailed off, unable to say the words, and stared up at the ceiling for a moment. I had a sneaking suspicion he was trying to stop himself from crying. "She needs to ask us a few questions."

Randall motioned for me to sit on the couch across from Heather, which I did gingerly. I pulled out a small notebook and a pen I'd found at home. I figured if I was going to be a professional at this, I should write down what I found out.

Randall took his place next to Heather, tenderly wrapping his arms around his wife and holding her close to him. He pressed his cheek against the top of her head. "I know it's hard, dear, but we have to go through this. It's important."

Heather nodded, wiping her eyes. She looked up at me, pressed her lips together, and gave a slight nod, as if steeling herself for what was coming. Her red-rimmed eyes were a startling shade of blue, and her skin was completely flawless. Given Jo's age, I had to assume she was at least in her mid-forties, but she could easily have passed for ten years younger than that.

"Charlotte. You look to be around the same age as my daughter. Did you know my Jo?"

"I never had the pleasure," I replied, shaking my head.

"Well, first and foremost, I want you to know she was kind. It's important that you know that. She loved animals. Her favorites were horses. She loved to ride more than anything in the world."

"Heather, Charlotte needs to ask us some questions. I'm sure she doesn't want to hear about what Jo's everyday life was like."

"It's fine, really," I said quickly, giving him a reassuring smile. For one thing, I understood Heather's need to speak about Jo. When Dad had died, I was afraid I would forget him. I was worried that one day, I would forget the feeling of the stubble on his face when he gave me a kiss on the cheek. That I would forget the way he squinted when he laughed as he faced the sun when he came back onto the beach. I wanted to tell everyone that would listen every single story I had about him while I still remembered them.

The more practical side of me also figured that the more I knew about Jo, the more avenues of investigation I would have to solve her murder.

"She loved horses. She kept one at a stable not far from here. His name is Joe. Jo and Joe." Heather managed a little laugh. "She was eight years old when she got him. Oh, how am I going to tell that horse that Jo is gone?"

Heather's eyes brimmed with tears once more, and Randall squeezed her hand hard. I figured now was as good a time as any to get started on questions. I hoped it would be less painful if I started with the easy stuff.

"What did Jo do for a living these days?"

"She worked for my company," Randall replied. "She went to UH and studied computer science with a minor in business administration. As soon as she finished, I hired her as an entry-level programmer, and she'd been moving up in the company. I was planning on grooming her to take over the business. She wanted to do it. I know so many parents that push their children into the family business, but Jo always loved computers and loved what I did. She wanted to take it over, and I was more than happy for her to do that one day."

"Was anyone at the company upset about the fact that Jo was the heir apparent? Maybe someone was bitter that you were bringing in a family member to take over?"

Randall shook his head. "No. At least, no one's ever come to me with concerns, and I've never heard any rumblings about it. I'm not saying it's impossible, but if it's happened, I'm not aware of it."

"Okay. I'll have to look at her office before anyone else gets to it."

"Of course. The police were there today. I can let you in tomorrow."

"Great. What about her personal life? I heard she recently broke up with her boyfriend."

Heather scowled, and I immediately knew what she thought of Tommy.

Randall's voice was ice cold when he answered. "Yes, and it was about time she did. We tried not to say too much. After all, it's her life, and she could live it the way she wanted to. She had to make her own mistakes. But let me tell you, when we found out she dumped him, we went out for dinner to celebrate."

"That man was trash. Pure trash," Heather added, venom in her voice. "He had no redeeming qualities, and as much as I loved my daughter, I just could not see what she saw in that man, no matter how hard I tried."

"I met him this afternoon," I said. "I completely agree with you."

"She said he understood her," Randall said with a shrug. "What can I say?"

"Do you think he might have killed her?"

"Frankly, I don't think he would have succeeded," Randall replied, the corner of his eye twitching. "The man never managed to finish anything in his entire life. He dropped out of high school after grade 11. He tried going back to community college to finish his degree and failed. He'd lost three jobs that I know of during the six months he was with Jo. No, I'm sure if he'd tried, he would have messed it up."

"You can't rule him out, Randy," Heather snapped at her husband. "If he wanted to kill her, he might well have done it. I don't know him well enough to say for sure, but statistically, he's most likely to be the killer."

I nodded in agreement. I was a big fan of true-crime murder podcasts and TV shows, and that was the reality: when women were killed, it was almost always by a partner or a former partner. The statistics were actually staggering. "I'm going to look into him very closely."

"Good," Heather said. "I can't think of anyone else who might have wanted to hurt her. But of course, Jo probably had problems she wouldn't tell me about. She was always a very independent young woman. I was so proud of her. But there are some things a daughter just doesn't want to talk to her mother about. She wanted me to think she had it all figured out. She wouldn't have told us if there was something really wrong."

"You don't think so?" Randall asked, his brow furrowing. "But we're her parents. We've always been there for her."

"I know, but she wasn't a little girl anymore," Heather said, putting a hand on her husband's knee for a second before swallowing back a small sob. "She was a grown woman, and she wanted us to see that. I don't think she would have told us about any problems she was having, but she would have told Casey."

"Who?"

"Casey Kahale. She was Jo's best friend," Heather explained. "She's a nurse now. She works at one of the clinics here in town. I can probably find out for you which one."

"Don't worry about it," I said quickly. "I'll find out." The last thing I wanted to do right now was to make more work for Heather Lismore.

She nodded.

"Well, I think that should do it for now," I said, standing. I didn't want to intrude on this family any more than I had to, and I certainly had a few good leads to get started with. "Thank you for your time. I know this must have been difficult for you."

"Just find the person who did this," Heather implored.

"I'm going to do my best."

Randall led me back to the front door. "Thank

you. It's a relief to know that you're here and that you're going to help."

"Of course. I'll be in touch."

"Thank you. And if you need an advance on any expenses, please let me know."

"I will."

As soon as I got into the car, I sent a text to the one person I knew could help me right now: Dot.

Hey. I need you to look someone up for me. Also, what do you know about Randall Lismore?

I drove off and heard the phone ping in the cupholder a moment later. As soon as I was stopped at a red light, I took a split second to glance at the reply.

Sure. Come on over and I'll tell you everything you need to know.

I smiled as I headed over to Dorothy's apartment.

Chapter 6

Dorothy lived in a somewhat older but well-cared-for building not too far from my mother's house in Kihei. While from the outside, the apartment looked like all the others, the inside of her place was unlike any home I'd ever seen.

A massive multiple-monitor setup took up the majority of the living room, with a giant bookcase filled with books on crime and technology filling up most of the rest of the main space. Her partner in crime Rosie answered the door, obviously expecting me.

"Hi," I greeted her warmly. "It's nice to see you."

"And you," Rosie replied, her big brown eyes crinkling at the corners as her round face broke out into a smile. "How have you been the last week?"

"Great, actually. Last night, Zoe and I looked at an apartment that we're going to rent from the mom of one of her coworkers. And I'm waiting on an email from the seller of a car I really like. It's a little over my budget, so I offered her five grand. Here's hoping they'll agree to it."

"Good," Dot called out from the living room, where I saw a flash of silver hair. "And if they don't, I'll roll up to the seller's place and break their knees."

I laughed. "Thanks. It's good to know you have my back."

"Anytime." The reality was that Rosie was much better suited to breaking knees than Dot. Dot had a lot of energy, but Rosie had been a trained agent of the USSR who defected after being assigned to spy for the Soviets in Honolulu. "Now, you said you wanted to know about Randall Lismore?"

I nodded. "Did you hear about the body that washed up on the shore last night?"

"Yes, it's his daughter," Rosie said, nodding solemnly. "Tragic. She was young, about your age."

"A few years younger, yeah. Anyway, because I was the one who received the reward from the James MacMahon murder, her father has hired me to look into his daughter's death."

"No kidding," Dot said, raising her eyebrows.

"Yeah. He's offering me a hundred grand if I solve it. Can I get help from you guys again, and if we solve this one too, we split it three ways—for real this time?"

Dot and Rosie exchanged a look. "Works for me," Dot said with a shrug. "The internet hasn't been as exciting as usual. You hack into one government department, it's like hacking into all of them. Boring. I'd much rather try and find a murderer."

"Me too," Rosie said. "If I'm honest, it was kind of a rush using the skills of my old life."

"Look at this old lady." Dot grinned. "She's tasted blood, and now she can't get enough."

"I don't mean *that*," Rosie scolded. "I mean using my brain. Sneaking around. The rush of adrenaline of knowing you're going to get in huge trouble if you get caught. I didn't realize just how much I'd missed it until I went through it again."

"All right, Agent 99. If the *Get Smart* people were on Team KAOS" Dot replied.

"I'm not on Team KAOS." Rosie glowered at her friend. "Anyway, long story short, yes, of course we'll help, Charlie."

"Great," I said with a laugh. "First thing we need to do is find Casey Kahale. She's a nurse and Jo Lismore's best friend. I didn't want to bother her family and make them find her contact information. Also, you guys are going to *love* Jo's ex-boyfriend, Tommy. Personally, I really hope he did it, because nothing would make me happier than throwing his disgusting ass in jail."

"Excellent," Dot said, turning to her computer and typing away. "What did you say that name was?"

"Casey Kahale."

"Give me a couple of minutes."

Ninety seconds later, Dot had an answer. "She works at Kihei Town Medical Clinic. Tomorrow, her shift is from ten until seven."

"Wow," I said, raising my eyebrows. "That was quick."

"Give me a minute," Dot said, tapping away. "Right. I've booked you in there for an appointment. I hope you come up with an ailment before tomorrow. If not, it sounds like Rosie will be happy to punch you in the nose for fun."

I laughed. "I think I'd rather come up with something a little less painful."

Dot shrugged. "Up to you. Make it something basic, though. Something that they'll send a nurse to look at rather than a doctor."

"So I can't pretend my liver is failing."

"No, that's probably outside the purview of a local family clinic."

I nodded. I was sure I would be able to come up with something. "Got it. When's my appointment?"

"Four. It's about two blocks from where you're working now, so you'll be able to get there in time."

"Good," I said, making a mental note.

"What did you say the boyfriend's name was? He should be the prime suspect."

"Oh, he is," I said. "All I have is a first name. Tommy. He'd be about Jo's age, if that helps at all."

"He's from the island?"

I shrugged. "Don't have a clue. Frankly, I'd be willing to bet the easiest way to find him is on Tinder."

Rosie laughed. "That kind of guy, hey?"

"He propositioned me immediately upon entering the ice cream shop today, telling me he was celebrating because his ex-girlfriend was dead."

"Even my old communist friends from back in the day didn't have that many red flags," Rosie muttered.

"Right? And somehow, the conversation got *worse* from there."

"Do you have any other suspects?" Rosie asked, and I shook my head.

"Not yet. I've only been on the case about twelve hours, and I spent most of those scooping ice cream. I also want to go have a look at her workplace. Jo was being groomed to take over the business when her father retired—completely willingly, according to him—but while he didn't know of anyone who was jealous about it, he also admitted it was unlikely anyone would come to him with concerns of that nature. I want to get a feel for what that place is like and what the employees really thought of Jo."

"Good call," Rosie said. "So she was in her family's business?"

"Yeah. Her father made his money online. Then apparently he sold the company, was set for life, and started another one, which is what he's doing now."

"Randall Lismore?" Dot asked.

I nodded. "Yeah. What do you know about him? You're into technology; surely you're up with the gossip."

"The official story is that sure enough, he started a company leading up to the dot-com bubble around the turn of the century. I don't know what the company did, and frankly, back then, it didn't really matter. You just had to start *something*, claim to be big on the internet, and you were swimming in VC money. But where Randall Lismore was smart was that he got out before it all came crashing down. He sold the company—I think they actually did make accounting software for businesses, but they weren't worth nearly their valuation—and found himself one of the richest men on Maui. Then he took that cash and invested it but decided retirement wasn't for him. He started a new company; this one makes simple apps for people's phones. They're trying to become the new *Angry Birds* or *Candy Crush*."

"Does it make any money?"

Dot shrugged. "Beats me. It's hard to tell with a lot of these things. Sure, the companies will put out press releases announcing their earnings, but they never mention how much they spent on advertising. And a lot will run at a loss, hoping that they eventually get that one big win that will make up for everything else. Randall might be at that stage. He certainly can afford to lose some money to start off with."

"What's the unofficial version?" Rosie asked. "You said that was the official line."

Dot grinned. "The unofficial version is a lot juicier and has a lot less evidence. *That* side of the story is that originally, Randall had a second partner in the first company. A friend of his from college. The partner died, supposedly in suspicious circumstances, but Randall was never charged. There were rumors floating around in some circles that Randall offed his partner. Randall immediately bought up the shares from the partner's widow then sold the company a few months later, not too long before the big crash finally came."

I let out a low whistle. "Well, that's not great."

"*If* it's true," Dot pointed out. "Randall was never charged, after all. The fact that he bought up the widow's shares and sold the company is true, and it can be considered a little sleazy, but there's certainly nothing illegal about it. The murder thing, though? I wouldn't have a clue."

"It would be good to know if he did it," I mused. "He seems like such a nice guy."

"A lot of psychopaths are," Dot said pointedly.

I nodded. "Oh, I know. People like Ted Bundy preyed on people believing that psycho killers were all obviously creepy and weird. They would invite him into their homes. Someone that friendly, that normal, could never be a bad dude! But of course, they were wrong, and there are countless examples just like that."

"Exactly." Dot gave me an approving look. "The thing most people don't realize is a lot of killers are hiding in plain sight."

"So if Randall did kill his business partner, it doesn't mean it's completely out of the question that he would kill his daughter, though it's a big jump from killing a friend to killing your offspring. The only question is: why? I don't have any motive for Randall to have done it, and without motive, I'm hard-pressed to keep him on a suspect list based on twenty-year-old rumors. I haven't got the answer to that just yet. Hopefully, tomorrow, after I visit the business, I'll have a better idea. He certainly played the role of the grieving father well, but again, it could just be an act."

"What about the mother? Did you meet her?" Rosie asked.

I nodded. "Yes. She didn't strike me as the type to kill her own daughter. She was obviously grief-stricken, and I don't think she was faking it. But again, I'm keeping an open mind, because you never really do know."

"Good. As you say, you'll find some suspects. And we'll help how we can."

"Is this the ex?" Dot asked from her chair at the computer, moving to the side to give me a better look at the monitor.

Sure enough, the guy staring back at me from the screen was Tommy. Dot had found his Facebook account. His profile picture was a shirtless selfie taken in front of his bathroom mirror, with Tommy flexing one arm to show off his muscles, grinning away. He had his sunglasses on despite being indoors, his shorts hung *way* too low for my comfort, and his hair had so much gel in it I imagined it could make the Leaning Tower of Pisa stand up straight.

"I can smell the Axe Body Spray through the monitor," I said, scrunching up my face. "That's him."

"And behind door number one is Thomas Gardner, who goes by Tommy," Dot said. "I keep a number of fake profiles ready and active just for situations like this, because men will almost always accept a friend request from a random woman wearing a bikini in her profile picture, regardless of whether or not they actually know her."

I snorted. "So you can see all his posts?"

"Sure can. And you're right, he seems to be a real winner. Most of what he posts on Facebook are memes involving the numbers 420 and 69. Also some thinly veiled references to the size of his manhood."

"Ah, yes, because everyone knows the guys with the biggest dongs always brag about it on social media," I said, rolling my eyes. "Is there anything on his profile that looks like it was posted by someone with an IQ in the double digits?"

"Not really," Dot muttered. "About two weeks ago, he made a post bragging about how he was single again and that if anyone wanted to slide into his DMs, he would be okay with that, as long as they're hot."

"What a great human being. I can't wait to meet him," Rosie said, rolling her eyes.

"Why can't people like *him* get murdered?" I said, earning myself a laugh from Dot.

"Well, I can't help you answer that, but he does have an employer listed here."

"I'm just going to go ahead and assume it's not a customer-facing role."

"You're correct. He works construction. Has Pono Contracting listed as his employer. I know the place; they did some work for the school a couple years before I retired, when they needed the plumbing upgraded. I don't think I saw this guy, though. Or at least, if I did, he had a shirt on."

"Trust me, he was memorable. If he had been working, you'd remember him."

"He doesn't exactly scream 'holds a job for long periods of time,' either," Rosie pointed out. "Either way, we'll look into him."

"Great," I said. "We reconvene tomorrow then?"

"Sounds good. I assume after your shift?"

I nodded. "Yeah. I'll text and let you know my schedule, since I also have to stop by Jo's office."

I left Dot's apartment and headed home. Things were slowly starting to come together.

Chapter 7

The following morning started off pretty well. I woke up to an email from the seller of the Jeep I coveted; she was willing to sell it to me for six grand. Okay, it was a *little* bit over my budget, but come on. I wasn't going to say no to a neon-blue Wrangler over a grand. I emailed back that I'd take it and gave her my phone number so we could organize a time to meet.

Then, as I was driving Mom's car down for what would hopefully be the last time to Aloha Ice Cream, my phone binged in my pocket. When I got to work, I checked it to find it was from Zoe.

The lease papers are ready for us to sign. I can bring them over tonight and we can take over the apartment tomorrow.

Great, I can't wait! I replied, my heart swelling with anticipation at having my own place again.

It wasn't that I didn't love my mom, I did, very much. And I would always be grateful to her for giving me a place to stay when I had been scared for my life in Seattle. But oh boy, was she a lot to handle sometimes. It would be nice to be able to occasionally be able to bring a guy home without my mom trying to sell him on my best features like an infomercial.

Especially when my selling features usually involved mentioning how good I would be at bearing children. And no grown woman wants to hear her mother tell a man how milkable her breasts are. Yes, that actually happened once. I almost melted into the floor.

I had a spring in my step as I walked through the front door of Aloha Ice Cream. Today was going to be a good day.

It got even better when the weather turned and we got a rare rainy day here on Maui. By one o'clock, when we had gone about twenty minutes without a single customer, Leslie turned to me. "You might as well head off and work on solving Jo's murder. There's no point in you being here."

"Thanks," I said gratefully. "I actually have a few other things I want to get done too."

"Do you want tomorrow off? It's fine with me if you do."

"Sure. Thanks, Leslie. I'll see you in a couple days."

"You just do your best to find that killer, will you? Jo was a nice kid. She deserves justice."

I nodded. "I will."

I left the shop to find a text from the woman selling the Wrangler, offering to meet me in a few hours. Perfect. I sent back a reply agreeing and decided I was going to visit Jo's workplace. Hopefully, I'd come out of it with a suspect or two.

ISLAND PALM GAMES WAS HEADQUARTERED ON LOLA Street in Kahului, the closest thing Maui had to a real city. Set in a low-rise but modern rendered-brick building in a light industrial area, the company's head-quarters were very low-key, with only a small sign on the door indicating that I had the right place.

But then, it wasn't the sort of place that got foot traffic.

I opened the front door and found myself facing a bored-looking receptionist typing away on her phone. Her dark-brown hair reached just past her shoulders, and her makeup was flawless. And I knew her instantly.

As soon as she looked up and spotted me, her hazel eyes flashed with anger. "Someone told me you were back in town. I hoped it was a lie."

I immediately recognized Natalie Cornell, the bully who had brought Zoe and me together when we were in elementary school. She'd been kicking sand into Zoe's face, so I gave her a mouthful of her own medicine. Literally.

"I'm sorry, who are you?" I said, doing my best to look confused. "I'm afraid I don't recognize you."

Petty? Sure. Worth it? Absolutely.

Natalie's face turned the shade of a tomato. "It's

Natalie. We grew up together. But then you always were a little slow."

"Oh," I said, nodding. "That's right. Natalie. I remember now. Well, it's good to see you haven't changed. I guess 'terrible person' wasn't something you grew out of but just part of your permanent personality."

Natalie narrowed her eyes at me. "Like you can talk."

"Wow, great comeback. I'm sure there are three-year-olds on the playground that look up to you and your epic burns."

"What the hell are you doing here, anyway? Shouldn't you be, I don't know, in an unemployment line somewhere or something?"

I flashed Natalie the biggest fake-sweet smile I possibly could. "Your boss invited me here. I'm supposed to talk to the staff about Jo, since he's hired me to solve her murder. But I guess he didn't think you were important enough to tell about that."

"You're lying," Natalie snapped.

"Call him and see," I said smugly.

Natalie's eyes darted to the phone as she decided what to do. If she actually *did* call her boss, she'd be doing what I told her to, which I knew would annoy her more than anything in the world. On the other hand, if she didn't confirm what I was there for and let me run amok in the office, she could get in trouble if I was lying.

Of course, I wasn't lying, but *she* didn't know that.

My lips curled into a smug smile as Natalie went to

the phone. She always brought out the worst in me. But hey, that was what happened when she spent almost our entire childhoods trying to bully me into submission. It had never worked, but nothing made me happier than ruining her day.

My childhood nemesis wouldn't look me in the eye while she mumbled into her phone, and the look she gave me when she hung up was one of pure hatred.

"Fine. You're not lying."

"Great," I said perkily. "So why don't I start with you? What did you think of Jo?"

"She was a whore who sucked up to anyone she thought could help her climb up the ladder of life. There. Is that what you want to hear?" Natalie crossed her arms in front of her as if defying me to disagree.

"Depends. Is it true?"

"Yeah, it's true. I'll deny it if you tell Randall I said that, though."

"So I'm just going to go out on a limb and assume you weren't friends."

"No, we weren't. She thought she was so much better than me because she had a job that involved more than answering phones and scheduling meetings. Oh, sure, in front of everyone else, she was always, 'Oh, Natalie, you're so helpful!' and, 'What would we ever do without you?' But whenever we were alone, she treated me like I was a piece of crap she'd stepped in on the sidewalk."

"Should I ask you if you killed her?" I asked.

Natalie scrunched up her face. "Of course I didn't kill her. I wasn't even on the island that night. I was visiting family in Kona and only got back this morning." She smirked. "I can get you my boarding passes if you want. You're not going to be able to pin this on me, no matter how much I bet you'd like to."

Well, she wasn't wrong there. Between Tommy and now Natalie, Jo seemed to have known more than one person I'd like to have seen rot in jail.

"I would like to see them," I said. "As much as I'd love to throw you in jail for this, the reality is I actually do want to find the person who really did it."

"I don't," Natalie replied, digging through her purse. A moment later, she shoved a couple of boarding passes at me. Sure enough, they corresponded with the times she'd given me, they'd been used, and they still had the tags for checked luggage on the back.

I handed them back to her. "Well, it's good to know you being a terrible person stops short of actually murdering someone. You say you don't want the killer found. Why not?"

Natalie shrugged. "Jo deserved it. She pretended to be so perfect, but she wasn't. She hung out with a bad crowd. And did you meet her ex-boyfriend yet?"

"Tommy?"

Natalie nodded. "He's disgusting."

"Well, it took almost thirty years, but it looks like the two of us finally agree on something."

"Dig deep enough into Jo's life and you'll find out it was nothing like what she pretended to her father."

"Fine. Give me some names. Who should I talk to?"

"Here? No one. Everyone who works here is a moron. Though if you tell Randall I said that, I'll deny it."

"I don't care what you say about your job or anyone who works here. I just want to find Jo's killer."

"Fine. But you're not going to get much here. Speak to her friends. Her real friends."

"And who might those be?"

"What, you think I'm going to do your whole job for you? Figure it out yourself."

I rolled my eyes. "Fine. But I still have to talk to the people who work here. Who did Jo work with the most?"

"She has a team. Because of course she does; she's the owner's daughter. Jonathan Keegan is her boss. Come on. I'll take you to him."

Letting out a huge huff as if it was an incredible hardship for her to have to do her job, Natalie got up and led me through a door to the main workspace. It was like a scene right out of *Silicon Valley*. I mean, I assumed so, anyway. I'd never actually watched that show.

The whole office space was open plan. There wasn't a single door leading to an office anywhere, only an open set of stairs that led up to a mezzanine level above, where I assumed the big bosses worked. On the main floor, where we now stood, desks were interspersed with beanbag chairs, ping-pong tables, a snack area, couches, and more. A basketball hoop hung on one of the walls, and a few errant balls lay here and there on the floor. One guy chatted away on his phone, pressing it between his ear and shoulder while he bounced a tennis ball rhythmically against the nearby wall, his feet propped up on his desk.

This place had "tech bros" written all over it. Natalie walked past a group of about six people huddled around a single computer and led me to a man in his forties. Completely bald, wearing a pair of trendy sunglasses and a form-fitting sweater, he reminded me of a slightly more fashionable David Cross.

As soon as he spotted Natalie, he looked up from the screen, whose desktop was an early 90s picture of Ghostface Killa. Because nothing screamed "rap gangster" like a middle-aged guy dressed in business casual working as an app developer.

"Hi, Jonathan. This is a private investigator Randall hired to look into Jo's death. You're supposed to answer any of her questions." Natalie smirked at me. "Here you go. Good luck."

I was tempted to flip her off as she left, but that wouldn't have been especially professional of me, and I was here doing a job. Instead, I looked over at Jonathan, who was in the middle of a staring contest with my cleavage. No wonder this was the guy Natalie had brought me to.

God, I hated her.

"Hi," I said to Jonathan. "I hear you were Jo's boss."

"That's right," he replied to my boobs, grabbing a fun-sized Snickers bar from the small bowl on his desk and popping it into his mouth.

I grabbed a chair from nearby and plonked myself down on it, crossing my arms in front of me so he was forced to look me in the eye. If this was what Jo had had to deal with at work every day, I felt sorry for her. That didn't seem to deter Jonathan, but whatever. If he wanted to get aroused by staring at my arm hair, so be it.

"It's such a tragedy that she's gone."

"I'm sure you're going to miss her... assets," I replied, unable to help myself. "What was she like here? Did she get along with everyone? Were there any issues with her being the boss's daughter?"

Jonathan grinned. "She got along with everyone just fine." I had a sneaking suspicion he was talking about more than just her personality. "As far as I know, no one ever had any problems with her."

"Really? Nobody felt a bit slighted that she was the boss's daughter and being groomed to take over the business?"

"Frankly, most coders aren't businesspeople, and they know it. They're more invested in their company stock options than rising to a management position. Jo was the other way. She could handle the code well enough, but her heart was set on managing. She was ambitious. Her parents were Hawaii rich; she wanted to be Elon Musk rich. But most of the guys here know they don't have that ability. Or Elon Musk's cool attitude and Twitter account."

"Right. Who worked under her?"

Jonathan motioned with his head toward the group still clustered around the one computer. "Them.

That's her whole team right there, currently trying to decide on graphics for the new app they're working on. Feel free to go speak with them if you'd like, but I'm telling you, no one here had a problem with Jo. She was a great worker and super hot."

"Well, I guess I should be grateful you put those in that order, at least," I replied, rolling my eyes.

"What am I supposed to do? Pretend to be a monk?"

"Or you could make the tiniest effort not to comment on the appearance of your female cowork- ers. You can think the words without saying them out loud, you know."

Jonathan gaped at me for a moment as if he had never considered that as an option.

I rolled my eyes, got up, and headed over to the group at the computer.

The mechanical sound of keyboard clacking immediately ceased as I approached. The group working over the computer reminded me of the little aliens in the *Toy Story* movies. They all seemed to move as one as the men looked over at me, eyes wide.

"Can we help you?" asked the man who had been doing the typing.

I glanced at the screen quickly; they were working on some sort of coding. On the black background was a bunch of white type that I didn't even pretend to understand.

"I'm told you're the group that worked with Jo," I said. "I'm investigating her death for her father, and I'd like to speak with each of you individually."

"Fine," the guy said. "I'll go first."

"Great. Is there somewhere quiet we can chat?"

He looked around. "Uh, not really. Maybe just the corner?"

"That'll do."

Chapter 8

The guy got up from his chair, and I followed him to a quieter part of the room. He was about six feet tall, skinny as a rail, wearing a plain gray T-shirt and jeans. His hair was plastered to his forehead, and he reminded me a little bit of Justin Long.

He ran his hand through his hair and sat down on a beanbag chair, motioning for me to take one near him, which I did.

"That sucks about Jo," he started. "She was nice. I liked her."

"She was your boss?"

"Yeah. We reported to her, she reported to Jonathan, and he reported to Randall. That was the hierarchy."

"And what's your name?"

"Kevin. Kevin McCaine."

"How long have you worked here?"

"About four years now. I started right out of the computer science program at UH."

"Did you have any issues with having a woman as your boss?"

Kevin snorted. "No. Unlike some of the morons who work here, I've actually interacted with women before and know that they are human beings just like me."

I gave him a small smile. "Anyone in particular?"

"Well, it can't have been comfortable for Jo spending the entire day working around someone who thought her face was a C-cup."

"Jonathan."

Kevin nodded. "Honestly, if it was me, I'd have gone to Randall and complained. But that wasn't Jo's style. She thought no one would respect her if she did that, and so she put up with it."

"Did she have problems with anyone here?"

Kevin glanced over at the rest of the team. "No, not really."

"Come on, man. You're not that good a liar. And if someone on your team really did kill her, do you really want to be coming to work every day and working with that person?"

"Okay, that's a good point. Talk to Evan. He has some issues when it comes to respecting women and didn't take well to being told what to do by Jo. Also, there was a guy who worked with us until about a month ago. Sean Sherman. I'd hunt him down. I could see him doing this."

"He had issues with Jo?"

"Sort of. Talk to him; you'll see."

"Do you know where I can find him?"

"Not a clue. Sorry."

That was fine. I would put Dot on that. She'd get me an address.

"Okay. Is there anything else you can tell me that you think might help me find Jo's killer?"

Kevin shifted in his beanbag chair. He was obviously uncomfortable.

"Look, whatever you tell me stays between us. I'm not trying to get anyone in trouble except the killer. If you tell me something you shouldn't, it's not going to go up the chain."

"Right. I'll deny this if you say it came from me."

"Got it. Consider it confidential."

"Sean had problems that affected his work that led to him being fired. Problems that went up his nose, if you know what I mean."

I raised my eyebrows. "Coke?"

"Yeah. And he got it from his boss."

Wow. That I was not expecting.

"You're kidding. Jo was dealing?"

Kevin nodded, looking around furtively as he lowered his voice. "Yeah. I don't know how many people here know about it. I saw them one night behind the building when I stayed late. There's no doubt at all that's what they were doing. I never said anything since, well, besides being my boss, she's the owner's daughter. I figured if it came down to her or me, I was much more expendable."

"Fair," I said, nodding. "Okay, thanks." This had to be what Natalie and Tommy had been hinting at when she had said Jo's life was nothing like what her parents thought.

"No worries. I do hope you find who did this. I did like Jo. She was good as far as bosses go. Not the best programmer, but she never pretended to be."

"Did anyone take offense at her being the heir apparent at the company?"

Kevin shrugged. "Not that I ever heard. Not really. Most of us are good at coding but know we'd be terrible managers. I know I would."

"Cool. Can you get Evan to come over next?"

"Sure. Good luck."

I smiled at Kevin, who got up off the chair and a moment later was replaced by another man. He looked to be about the same age as Kevin, maybe an inch or two shorter, with just the very beginnings of a beer belly. His eyes were small and set deep into his face.

"You're investigating Jo's death?" Evan asked, and I nodded.

"Yeah."

"Well, you're wasting your time talking to me. I don't know anything about who killed her."

"Where were you the night she died?"

"I don't want to say."

"I mean, that's up to you, but I promise I don't care, and if you don't tell me, I have to continue to assume you're a suspect."

Evan snorted. "Whatever. I didn't kill the bitch."

"It sounds like you were on great terms. Why do you call her that?"

"Because that's what she was. Jo thought she was better than me because her daddy started the company. You know, she had no idea how to code. Couldn't tell a string of Python from C++. But we all had to pretend she knew what she was doing because daddy wanted her to take over the business. Do you see any other women on this floor? No, of course you don't. Do you know why?"

"Because the stench of BO is overwhelming?" I suggested.

Evan scoffed at me. "It's because women aren't smart enough to be coders. No offense."

"Oh yeah, how could I possibly take offense from *that* statement?"

"Yeah, well, it's true. Coding needs a logical brain, a mathematical brain. Women don't have that."

"Ah, yes, math, that famous field that's never had any women in it. Who are Hypathia, Ada Lovelace, and Katherine Johnson anyway? I guess no one knows, and in a hundred years, people will still be talking about Evan Smalldick instead."

"That's not my last name," Evan scowled. "Anyway, I don't know who those people are."

"Wow, now who doesn't know about computer coding? Seeing as Ada Lovelace basically invented it, you should be embarrassed."

Back in maybe fifth or sixth grade, Zoe had had a book on female scientists. I, of course, had completely forgotten my book for silent reading one day, so Zoe let me borrow hers. It was too short, and I ended up reading the entire thing through about four times before we were finally allowed to put our books down, but as a result, I had the names of those women imprinted directly onto my brain.

"Whatever. I don't have to answer to you."

"You do if you want to keep your job. And right now, if you want to stay out of jail. Because you're pretty high up on my list of people who might have wanted Jo dead right now."

"I told you, I have an alibi."

"Sure. But you haven't told me what that alibi is, genius."

"That's because I don't want to. Can't you just trust me?"

"Yeah, I'll totally take your word for it that you're not a killer. What is wrong with you? Of course not. Just tell me where you were. For what it's worth, I don't actually *care*."

Evan's face reddened. "I had a friend over."

"The whole night?"

"The whole night."

"Okay, buddy, you got laid. Nothing to be embarrassed about if you're not twelve. What's her name?"

"Katrina. I'll get you her phone number."

A moment later, I had the number in my phone, wondering what on earth Evan was so evasive about.

"Did you know Sean who used to work here?"

"Yeah, of course I did."

"What did you think of him?"

Evan shrugged. "He was strung out all the time. Frankly, I'm surprised he lasted as long as he did. Eventually, he got fired because his work was terrible.

Got what he deserved. I didn't keep in touch with him."

"Who do you think killed Jo?"

"No clue. It's not like I went out of my way to be close to her. She was my boss. I don't think it was anyone here if that's what you're asking. Most of the guys fawned over her like she was the first person with a pair of boobs they've ever seen. It certainly wasn't because her work was good."

"Right. Thanks. Can you get someone else to come over? I'm talking to the whole team."

Evan nodded and got up from the chair.

AN HOUR LATER, I'D SPOKEN TO THE REST OF JO'S team and gotten no further in terms of understanding who might have wanted her dead. No one else seemed remotely close to her personally, and none of them seemed to have the same enlightened attitude about women as Evan.

"So, do you know who did it yet?" Natalie asked with a smirk as I headed back to the reception area in order to leave.

"Not yet. Was it the coke dealing you were hinting about before?"

Natalie's smirk quickly fell off her face, turning into a scowl. "Seriously, you found out about it? Which one of those nerds actually figured it out?"

I ignored the question. "Do you have contact information for Sean Sherman?"

"I guess so. We had to mail him his last check. Give me a minute."

Sighing loudly, as if I was really messing up Natalie's day, she scribbled an address down onto a Post-it note and held it out to me. I grabbed it, slipping it into my purse.

"Are you really staying on the island for good this time?" Natalie asked.

I nodded. "Yeah. I hope I don't see you around."

"Likewise."

I left the building then, checking the time. There were still a couple of hours left before I had to be at the clinic for my medical appointment, but I had half an hour before I was meeting the woman with the Jeep. Perfect timing.

Chapter 9

I'd organized to meet the woman selling me her Jeep in the parking lot of a large strip mall on South Kihei Road, not far from Aloha Ice Cream. I had the cash ready to go, and as soon as I spotted the car, I fell in love.

She was just as beautiful as in the ad. The sunlight glinted off the neon-blue exterior, contrasting beautifully with the black parts.

"Charlie?" the woman asked. She was tall, well over six feet, with blond hair tied back into a ponytail, dressed in no-nonsense jeans and a black tank that showed off arms so tanned I imagined she spent half her life in the sun.

I nodded, reaching out to shake her hand. "That's me. Olivia?"

"Yup. You're going to love this car. It's served me well over the years, and I've done a whole bunch of work on it."

"You're a mechanic?"

Olivia nodded. "The best on the island. You have any problems, you come to me, you hear?"

"Got it," I said with a grin. This was perfect; if Olivia was a mechanic I didn't even need to get it inspected, really. She seemed honest enough. We exchanged cash and title, and before I knew it, I had the top down, driving down South Kihei Road in my new Jeep, wearing a huge grin as the wind whipped my hair around my face.

Everything was coming up Charlie.

I STILL HAD A COUPLE HOURS TO GO BEFORE I HAD to be at the clinic for my appointment, so I decided to grab a quick lunch. I found a café advertising the best Loco Moco on the island, and I couldn't resist. It had been literally years since I'd enjoyed the dish, and my mouth watered at the thought.

A few minutes later, I was sitting on the beach with a compostable container filled with Hawaii's best comfort good.

Loco Moco was started on the Big Island back during World War II. Basically, you started with a base of rice, topped it with a hamburger patty and a fried egg, and slathered it with gravy. Nowadays, there were plenty of ways to fancy it up, but I had always been a fan of the traditional version. I wolfed it down while watching the waves, the salty ocean breeze wafting over my face. I was going to have to come down and have a swim in the ocean soon. The waters beckoned me, the siren call of the waves irresistible. No wonder so many people moved to Maui. Even at this time of year, the water was still plenty warm enough for swimming.

My lunch finished, I pulled out my phone and dialed the number for Katrina, Evan's paramour, to confirm his alibi.

The number rang a couple of times before clicking over to a voice mailbox. The voice on the other end of the introductory message was soft and sultry, reminding me a lot of the ads for phone-sex hotlines from the late nineties.

"Hi, sweetie. You've reached Katrina. If you've been a bad boy and need to be punished, leave your name and number, and I'll get back to you when I think you deserve it."

I burst out laughing right there at the picnic table. No wonder Evan had been so hesitant to give me his alibi. Katrina was a dominatrix for hire.

When I heard the low-frequency beep telling me it was time to record my message, I did so.

"Hi, Katrina. This is Charlie Gibson. I'm investigating the murder of Jo Lismore. One of your clients, Evan, gave me your number as his alibi, and I'm wondering if you could give me a call back to either confirm or deny. Thanks, and, um, happy dominating?"

Great. At least I hadn't ended that call *super* awkwardly. I rolled my eyes at my own complete and total lack of social skills and got up, throwing out the container from my lunch and the can of Coke Zero that I'd had with it.

I SPENT THE REST OF THE TIME TEXTING DOT AND Rosie. We organized to meet at Dot's place and have dinner, and before I knew it, I was standing in front of Kihei Town Medical Clinic. The low-rise building looked the same as any other place in a strip mall, with stenciled lettering on the window announcing the business name, along with a red cross underneath.

"Good, you're here," a voice next to me said, and I found Dot standing by my side.

"I thought we weren't meeting until after."

"Sure, but I decided I wanted to meet the best friend myself. Besides, it's not like I have anything else to do today."

"Right," I said, opening the door and holding it for Dot. Heading to the counter, I gave my name to the receptionist, who handed me a clipboard and pen with a sheet to fill out with my basic personal and medical information.

"So, what did you come up with?" Dot asked as she peered over the sheet of paper as I filled in my medical history.

I frowned at her and covered the sheet with my hand like we were in school and she was trying to cheat off me.

"What, you're afraid I'm going to see you had chicken pox when you were a kid? Trust me, Charlie,

I'm nearly eighty. There's not a single thing on that sheet that can scare me. I've seen it all, and I've had friends die from it all."

Well, I couldn't argue with that. "Fine, if you *must* know, I had mono when I was a teenager. I drank from a friend's water bottle who had it."

Dot snorted. "Is that all?"

"It's the principle of the thing! You're not supposed to peek at someone's medical history. And to answer your question, I was thinking of saying I was getting pain in my lower back. That's what kidney stones feel like, right?"

Dot nodded. "Good thinking. And I'm nosy. I can't help it. It's in my nature."

"Yeah, well, you could always just sneak looks at your neighbor out the window like a normal person," I muttered.

"That's no fun. Besides, if you don't tell me, I'll just hack their database again later and find out everything I need to know for myself."

"Isn't the Department of Defense much more interesting than my medical history, anyway?"

"Oh, much. But that doesn't mean I don't want to see them both."

I finished filling out the form and handed it back to the receptionist then went back to sit with Dot in the waiting area. Most of the seats had been taken at this point. An older woman casually browsed a back issue of *Better Homes and Gardens*, while an exhausted-looking pregnant woman casually scrolled through an app on her phone as her other child, a boy of maybe two or three years old, crashed the giant Lego blocks in the corner that served as a play place into one another. A couple of teenagers and an older man finished off the small waiting area.

"So what did you find out this morning?" Dot asked.

I gave her a quick rundown of what I'd learned at Jo's place of work.

"Hm. I wasn't expecting 'secretly a drug dealer' to come out of that, but at least it gives us a good avenue of inquiry."

"I'm still hoping it was the ex."

"Me too, really. He sounds like a peach. I can't wait to meet him."

"Charlotte Gibson?" a nurse called from the doorway.

I stood up, and so did Dot. I shot her an exasperated look. "Seriously?"

"What? You never know how I can help. Besides, it's not like you've *actually* got kidney stones."

"Fine," I muttered, shaking my head and following the nurse, clutching at my back to make it look like I really was in pain. Her nametag read "Amanda," so she obviously wasn't who we were looking for.

She led Dot and me to a small, windowless room that looked like every single other doctor's office in the country. Plain white walls, with a poster of the cardio-vascular system across from a firm-looking medical bed covered in a white sheet. Next to the bed was a chair, which Dot immediately claimed for her own, leaving me to perch myself awkwardly on the edge of the bed, trying not to make the covering crinkle loudly.

I wasn't exactly a fan of doctor's visits, and the fact that I had completely made up an ailment in order to meet one of the nurses here didn't help. However, a moment later, when a woman walked in with "Casey" written on her name badge, I pushed all that aside.

"Hi, Charlotte?" she said, offering me a smile. Casey was on the shorter side, maybe five foot three on a good day, of medium build, with her straight brown hair tied back in a ponytail. Obviously friendly and efficient, Casey immediately reminded me of exactly what a nurse should be like.

"That's me."

"Right. I'm just going to take your temperature and blood pressure. You've come in with back pain?"

"Yeah," I said. "It started last night and hasn't gone away. It's not so bad that I need to go to emergency, but I figured I'd get it looked at anyway."

"Good thinking," Casey replied as she grabbed the blood pressure strap off the wall. "We'll get you all taken care of here."

"Thanks. Listen, while I have you, are you the Casey who was best friends with Jo Lismore?"

Casey gave me the side-eye while she wrapped the blood pressure monitor around my arm. "You're not some kind of journalist, are you?"

"No," I replied. "Randall Lismore hired me to find out who killed her. You can call him and ask if you'd like."

"Randall?" Casey scoffed. "Sorry, I have no interest in helping him."

"You would be helping Jo," I said quickly, and Casey's expression fell. "Come on. Help me out. I was told you were her best friend. No matter who hired me, it's the best thing for Jo if I find out who killed her, right?"

Casey pursed her lips, considering my words as she began inflating the tube, stethoscope pressed just above the crease in my elbow.

"Why don't you like Randall, anyway?"

"He didn't want what was best for Jo. He never did."

"Oh? He pushed her into computer science?"

Casey nodded. "He always pretends that Jo really wanted to do it, that she saw him running the company growing up and wanted to be involved. It was total bull. Jo wanted to be a vet. She loved animals more than anything. But Randall wouldn't pay for it. He said it was ridiculous. He said veterinary school was too competitive. He told Jo he would pay for her to go to business school or learn computer science. That was it."

"So she did it."

Casey shrugged. "What else was she supposed to do? Without her parents' support, she wouldn't have any way to pay for veterinary school, especially since she would have had to go to the mainland to do it. So she did what her father wanted her to."

"And she wasn't happy?"

"Not at all. She made lists of all the people at that

company she wanted to fire as soon as she took over. Her boss, Jonathan, was at the top of the list."

"Having met the guy, I can understand why."

"Right? Like, buddy, my eyes are up here." Casey rolled hers while she deflated the strap around my arm and marked the numbers down on the page. "No, Jo hated that job."

"Funny, Randall made it out as if she was happy. Most of her coworkers seemed to like her too."

"That was the thing about Jo. She was really good at faking it. But she had her ways to get back at her family."

"Tommy? Please tell me she wasn't *actually* attracted to him."

Casey scrunched up her face in disgust. "Goodness, no. Honestly, how she stayed with that creep for so long is beyond me. But it annoyed her parents to no end. That was the goal."

"And the drug dealing?"

Casey's arms fell to the side as she gave me a hard look. "What drug dealing?"

"You didn't know?"

Casey shook her head, her brow furrowing slightly. "No. There's no way. I would have known."

"Someone saw her doing it."

"They must have seen something else. I'm telling you, Jo wasn't into that sort of thing. And if she was, she would have told me."

"Okay," I said. "Who do you think could have killed her?"

"Honestly, I bet it was that guy she fired."

"Do you mean Sean Sherman?"

Casey nodded. "That's the name, yeah."

"Jo was the one who fired him?"

"Randall thought she should get experience in all parts of business, including firing people. She was so nervous about it too. She called me that morning. She felt like she was going to throw up."

"I can imagine," I murmured.

"It didn't help that it went pretty terribly. Sean didn't take the firing well. Called Jo a whole bunch of nasty names. Eventually, she had to call the cops to get him escorted off the premises."

"No kidding."

"Yeah. It was bad. She'd waited until everyone else had gone home, but her father stayed behind just in case. It was a good thing he was there. I don't know what Sean would have done if they were alone." Casey shook her head. "So yeah, if you ask me who killed her, he'd be at the top of my list."

"What about Tommy?"

Casey scoffed. "If that—I hesitate to call him a man—that *thing* had any sort of backbone at all, maybe. But he's all show. Doesn't have an ounce of courage in him."

I barked out a laugh. "That sounds about right."

"Jo didn't even like him. She just like that he annoyed her parents."

"Why did they break up?"

"I think she just got sick of him. He said something disgusting one time too many, and Jo decided it wasn't worth it anymore. So she kicked him to the curb."

"Do you know what she was doing the night she was killed? If she had any plans?"

"I spoke to her that evening," Casey said. "We had made plans to go shopping together on the weekend. She told me she just planned on spending a quiet evening inside. Then when I found out the next day…" Casey's voice trailed off as her eyes welled with tears, but she blinked them back. "I found out around noon. I wish I could tell you what she was doing. All I know is what the police told me: she died between ten and eleven that night. If only we'd gone out together. We probably would have still been at the club then."

"Okay, thanks," I said. "Can I give you my phone number? If you think of anything else, let me know, okay?"

"Fine. I guess it doesn't matter who you're working for. Randall can't do anything more to her now. Just find who did this, will you? Bring them to justice. Whoever it was, Sean or someone else, I want them to pay for what they did to Jo. She was a nice person. She didn't deserve this."

"We'll do our best," I replied.

"Okay. The doctor will be here in just a minute."

And with that, Casey left. I couldn't help but hear that her voice had gone a little husky as she was leaving. She had been brave the whole time we spoke, but she was obviously grieving for her friend.

Chapter 10

A few minutes later, the doctor entered. The man, about fifty with dark-brown hair just beginning to gray at the ends, had a no-nonsense expression, giving each of us a curt nod as he walked in and took his spot at the tiny doctor's desk, opening the file.

"Charlotte Gibson. I'm Dr. Yeller. You're complaining of back pain?"

"That's right," I said, reaching for my lower back. "It started last night, right around here."

Dr. Yeller tapped lightly where I mentioned. "Does that hurt?"

"A little," I replied, hoping it was the right answer. We went through a few more questions, and he sat down and looked at me.

"It's likely you have a kidney stone, although you'd have to get an ultrasound to be sure. Right now, since the pain seems manageable it's likely not stuck. I can give you a prescription that can help you pass it more easily. He pulled out a notepad and began scribbling on it.

"Can you give her something a little stronger in case the pain gets worse?" Dot asked.

"I can write you a prescription for naproxen," Dr. Yeller replied.

"How about some oxy? Or at least T3s?"

Dr. Yeller gave Dot a disapproving glance. "I'm afraid we don't prescribe opioids at this clinic at all. You'll have to see your regular family doctor for that or go to emergency. Besides, so long as it appears the stone will be passing on its own, there's no need for more aggressive pain management."

"Sorry, just ignore her. My grandmother doesn't know what she's saying anymore," I replied, shooting daggers at Dot.

"I know exactly what I'm saying," Dot replied. "I might be old, but I haven't lost it just yet."

"Sure thing, Grandma. You know you're not supposed to watch those TV shows late at night." I shot Dr. Yeller an apologetic look. "She likes shows like *The Wire* and *The Sopranos*. I think they give her ideas."

"I have an idea. Why don't I wring your neck right here?"

"See?" I said, shaking my head sadly. "She takes it way too seriously. Thank you very much. I'll take the pills to make the stone easier to pass."

"All right," Dr. Yeller said, nodding solemnly while Dot ran her finger across her throat at me behind him. I pointedly kept my eyes on the doctor, ignoring

Dot. "I also recommend drinking a lot of water to help the stone pass. Ten to twelve cups a day should be your goal, or about two and a half to three quarts."

"Great, thanks."

"Is there anything else I can help you with today?"

I shook my head.

Dr. Yeller tore the prescription off his pad, handed it to me, and left with another curt nod.

When the door closed behind him, I glared at Dot. "What do you think you were doing?"

"I was testing him!"

"Testing him for what? To see if he would give you some stronger drugs?"

"Of course I was. You never know. Besides, people are so quick to write off the elderly as just being crazy. Did you see how easily he took your reasoning that I was just an old kook?"

"Sure. But what would you have done if he'd said yes?"

"Filled the prescription and kept it for the next time I was in pain," Dot said with a wink.

I shook my head at her incredulously. "Okay. Come on, let's get out of here. We have to meet Rosie anyway."

We headed to the parking lot, and when Dot realized what car we were headed for she let out a low whistle. "Now *that's* a beautiful car."

"Thanks," I replied with a grin. "She's my new baby. Cost me six grand."

"Good for you," Dot said approvingly. "That's a

decent price, and I'm glad you didn't go out and blow all your money on a new Bimmer."

"The Jeep's more my style than a BMW anyway. She needs a name."

Dot frowned. "She does need a name. And it can't be just anything. This car isn't an Agatha."

"No, you're right. She needs a name that's as cool as she is."

"I'll think about it. How about Thunderstruck? Like the AC/DC song?"

I nodded slowly. "That could work. That's certainly a cool name. Or maybe Lightning McQueen? I could call her Queenie for short."

"Isn't that the name of the main car in that animated movie?"

"*Cars*? Why yes, yes it is. But he's speedy and cool."

"He's also red. She's blue."

"I guess I just don't see car color like you do."

Dot rolled her eyes. "Fine. It could work. It has punch. I like Queenie."

"Queenie it is. I tapped the dashboard a few times as I turned the key in the ignition, and the engine turned over. "All right, girl. Take us to Dot's place."

I was just sliding Queenie into a parking spot when the phone rang in my pocket. Seeing it was Randall, I motioned for Dot to hold on a minute and answered.

"Hi, Randall," I greeted him.

"Hello, Charlotte. Charlie. How is your investigation going? I heard you were at the office today."

"I was," I replied. "I have a few leads to follow from there, which I'm going to do over the next day or two. I was wondering if it's possible to access Jo's apartment."

"That's the reason I was calling. The police have finished looking through it and told me I'm free to do as I wish with it. I can have the keys dropped off immediately."

"That would be great. I'm actually working on the case now at a friend's home. Would you mind dropping them off here?" I gave him Dot's address.

"Excellent. You'll have them in hand, with Jo's address, in twenty minutes."

"Thank you, Randall."

"Thank you for taking this so seriously. I spoke to the two detectives on my daughter's case this morning. I told them you're working on it separately and that I'd like them to keep you in the loop when they can. They weren't very pleased."

"No, I can't imagine they would have been."

"They told me they couldn't allow you access to anything they have. I hope that's not a problem for you."

"It's fine. I'll work around them as best I can. So far, I've got a few avenues I want to follow, and I hope to make some quick progress for you."

"Great. Thank you. Heather is not handling this well. I really want to have closure for her as soon as possible."

"I'm going to do my best," I assured Randall.

I said goodbye and hung up the phone then turned to Dot. "I hope you're ready for another adventure."

"Always."

We headed upstairs, where Rosie was already in the apartment, sitting on the couch and casually reading a book on blood spatter theory she'd found in Dot's bookcase.

"I thought Dot's place was protected like a fortress," I said when I saw Rosie.

"Oh, Rosie has access," Dot replied. "She's the only one I trust."

"Fair enough." The two old women were basically inseparable anyway; I wasn't especially surprised by the news.

While we waited for the keys to be dropped off, Dot and I caught Rosie up on what we'd discovered.

"Well, we have a few suspects, and also, it turns out Dot is probably a drug addict."

"Oh, I am not," Dot huffed.

"You tried to get oxy for my nonexistent kidney stones!"

"I tried to see if the doctor would prescribe it for you. There's a difference."

"And what reason would he *possibly* have to do that?"

"How should I know? But I wanted to check. I was curious."

"You know what they say about curiosity and the cat."

"Well, cats don't usually live to my age, so I think my curiosity is treating me pretty well."

"Yes, congratulations on not annoying anyone so much they've murdered you yet."

"Thank you."

I resisted the urge to roll my eyes so far into the back of my head they got stuck. Dot could be impossible sometimes.

Rosie laughed good-naturedly. "So we've discovered that there's a random doctor out there who won't give Dot any prescription she wants. What about the real suspects?"

"Well, apparently, Tommy doesn't have the stones to actually kill anyone, but I still don't want to cross him off my suspect list," I said, holding out one finger.

"Agreed," Dot said with a nod.

"I want to speak with Sean Sherman. And probably look him up first. A drug addict who got fired by his hookup might be unhinged enough to do something stupid." I held out a second finger and then a third. "And I don't like Jonathan, her boss. I think he was hiding something. In fact, it appears a lot of people in this case are hiding things."

Rosie flashed me a small smile. "You can't expect all murder cases to be easy to solve."

"Well, a girl can dream. Hopefully something in Jo's home will tell us who the killer is. And we can take my new car to get there."

"A new car, hey?" Rosie asked.

Dot grinned. "You're going to love it."

"WELL, IT STANDS OUT," ROSIE SAID WITH A LAUGH as soon as we reached the parking lot.

A man had come by a couple of minutes earlier

and handed me an envelope with a set of keys in it, along with an index card on which was written an address in Wailea, and the three of us had immediately headed out. Rosie took the passenger seat while Dot climbed into the back.

I punched the address into my phone and let out a low whistle. "Jo was living large. She's up on the hill above Wailea, just behind the golf course."

"Those are some pricy properties," Dot agreed. "But of course, coming from that family, I wouldn't expect anything else."

I nodded and put the car into gear. About ten minutes later, we pulled up in front of the building where Jo lived. I followed the signs for visitor parking, and we made our way along the rows and rows of apartments. The complex was obviously well cared for, with meticulous landscaping, plenty of shrubbery offering copious amounts of shade, and a freshly pressure-washed path that meandered in slow waves between the buildings.

Number 207 was a ground-floor apartment. The building's exterior was made of white rendered brick, probably built in the late nineties or maybe the early two thousands, going by the architectural style. The front door still had residue from the seal that had been left by the police.

I carefully unlocked the door and stepped inside. The bones of the place were pretty nice. The kitchen was modern, the walls a nice cream color and the floors a beautiful natural hardwood. I couldn't say too much for the rest of it. Either the police had left this place in complete shambles, or someone else had been here after them.

I turned to Rosie. "Did the cops do this?"

She pursed her lips. "I don't have a lot of experience with local law enforcement, but it would surprise me. They tend to be messy but not *this* messy."

Dot immediately walked through the living room to the patio door then checked the window next to it. "This window's been jimmied open. Someone was definitely here."

My phone chose that instant to buzz, and I pulled it from my pocket to see who was calling. It was Jake. He probably wanted to talk about Randall letting him know I was working on the case as well.

I pressed the volume down button to silence the ringer and stuck the phone back in my pocket.

"We should tell the cops," I said. "But not until we've had a look through here ourselves."

"That's if there's going to be anything left to find," Dot said, kicking idly at an errant throw cushion that had been strewn across the floor. "We're what, the third set of people to come through here now? Odds are anything good has already been taken by either the cops or whoever else came in here."

"Sure," Rosie said with a smile. "But there's a good chance whoever broke into this place was also Jo's killer."

I grimaced. "I never even considered that."

"Luckily for you, I did." Rosie pulled a small tool kit from her purse and opened it up. In it was a container of black powder, a small brush, and transparent strips.

"You have your own fingerprint-taking kit?"

"Of course I do," Rosie replied as if it was the most natural thing in the world. "I've been doing it since I got here."

Right. *I* was the weird one, the person who didn't carry a miniature forensic tool kit with me at all times.

"If you find something, I can get access to the fingerprint database," Dot said. "We'll find out who did this and hopefully find our killer."

"Okay, you guys take fingerprints. I'm going to look around and see if whoever went through this place left some sort of other clue as to who might have killed Jo."

"Take these," Rosie said, reaching into her bag and tossing me a pair of latex gloves. Because of course she had those on her too.

I slipped them on and went down the short hallway to the bathroom, which was on the left, across from the master bedroom. It was small, and every inch of the counter was taken up by some sort of hair product, face cream, or makeup item. Even the top of the toilet was home to a couple half-empty shampoo bottles.

It was hard to tell if the bathroom had been ransacked or if it always looked like this, but if I was a betting woman, I'd have said the latter. Despite the fact that it looked haphazard, there was actually some sort of order to the chaos if I looked closely. Jo was obviously a woman who cared about her appearance.

All of her makeup had been at least partly used, and it was good-quality stuff too. Most of it came from Sephora and MAC. I was on more of a Maybelline budget myself.

Opening the medicine cabinet, I was greeted by an industrial-sized bottle of Advil, half a pack of Claritin, and a tube of antibiotic cream. Nothing that seemed particularly out of place. I was about to close the door when I paused and grabbed the bottle of Advil. Popping the lid, I poured some of the pills from the bottle into my hand—and grinned.

This wasn't ibuprofen at all.

Chapter 11

The tiny white pills in my palm didn't look a thing like Advil. Plus there were other hints. Like the engraved "Percocet" around the rim on one side and "DuPont" written across the center of the other.

I peered into the bottle. Sure enough, it was filled to the brim with the same white pills.

"I think I've got something over here," I called out into the hall, and a moment later, the tiny bathroom was packed with the three of us.

I held out my hand to show the pills to the others.

"Well, that'll kill your headache all right," Rosie said with a chuckle.

"Sure, but you won't poop for a week," Dot said.

I took a deep breath and tried not to think about how *that* was the side effect Dot decided to point out. "This might be what the person who broke in here was after."

"I'm surprised the cops didn't find it," Rosie

mused. "Even if it was hidden in a bottle of Advil, they probably should have checked that."

"If it was the same cop as tried to Taser me, no chance," Dot said, shaking her head. "He'd need an IQ higher than his shoe size to manage that."

"Okay. What should we do with these?"

"I'll take them," Dot suggested, opening her hand.

I narrowed my eyes at her and pulled the bottle out of reach. "Not a chance, druggo."

"Why don't you hang onto them for now," Rosie suggested. "Show them to Zoe to confirm they're real, maybe?"

"If you give me one, I can tell you if they're real," Dot said with a wink.

"That's why *you're* not getting the bottle," I replied. "Rosie's right. I'll take them to Zoe. Did you find any fingerprints yet?"

"A single thumbprint," Rosie replied. "I'm not sure we'll have enough to get a solid match, but you never know. I want to see if the person touched the window on the exterior as well."

"Okay. I'll keep looking in here. If she hid some pills in this bottle, you never know where there might be more of them."

"Good call."

Rosie and Dot went back into the hall while I opened the cabinet under the sink and began digging through it. Where would I hide a bunch of drugs if I didn't want anyone to accidentally find them? Then my eyes landed on the box of Tampax. I grinned.

Grabbing the box, I dumped the contents into my

hand. Sure enough, the thin white paper sleeves that normally held tampons were now packed with more of those same white pills. I grabbed the box and headed into the living room. I waved it in the air at the others. "I found something you *definitely* don't want to shove up your hoo-ha."

"Is that what you young 'uns are calling it these days?" Dot asked with a grin. "Let me guess: more drugs?"

"Percocet again. Looks like Jo decided to specialize."

"Okay. Let's get out of here. I didn't find any more prints," Rosie said.

"And I searched the rest of this place. Nothing that might indicate who killed Jo. No phone or laptop. I'll try and get into anything she had online. The cloud is a godsend for hackers. You no longer need physical access to the drives when everything is online."

"Well, that's a disconcerting thought."

"It should be. Never keep anything on the cloud you don't want the NSA to see. Or me."

The three of us left the apartment, and I locked the door after us, slipping the key back into my purse.

"Seeing as we have enough drugs on us to get convicted of trafficking, try not to draw any attention to yourself as we head home," Rosie suggested as we reached the car. She eyed Queenie up and down. "Well, maybe not any more attention than you normally would."

I snickered. "Shouldn't be a problem."

It was getting late now; the sun had set, and I had

to drop Dot and Rosie off and get back to Mom's place to meet Zoe so I could sign the papers for the lease. I sent Zoe a quick text that I'd be home in half an hour. Her reply came through a moment later.

No problem. My shift at work doesn't start for another few hours. See you soon!

I smiled and climbed into the car. I was hoping I could get home with a car full of drugs without getting pulled over.

"Just so you know, if the cops get us, I'm making a run for it," Dot said as I pulled back onto the road.

I snorted. "Yeah, I'm sure you'll get super far."

"Like you can talk."

"Please, if we get caught, I'm blaming it all on you. And they'll believe me if you're running away."

"Ideally, none of us will get caught at all, because you're going to drive like a normal person who obeys the road rules, including the speed limit," Rosie said.

"I usually like to think of it as more of a suggestion than a hard limit, but tonight, I'm with you," I replied as we headed down the road.

Unfortunately for my plans on being a law-abiding citizen, as soon as I took a left onto Wailea Ike Drive to get back to the main road, some idiot pulled in behind me, decided I was driving too slowly, and put his high beams on.

"It's a two-lane road, moron," I called out. "Go around!"

He couldn't hear me, but yelling at him made me feel better anyway.

Rosie frowned from her spot in the passenger seat,

glancing in her side mirror. "Dot, see if you can get the license plate number off that car."

"It's probably just some idiot tourist who doesn't know the roads and is in a rush," I muttered.

"I'm not so sure," Rosie said quietly.

Her demeanor made me nervous, and I dared a glance back at the car in the rearview. It wasn't a car, actually. It was an SUV or maybe a truck. I couldn't quite make it out, what with the high beams searing into my eyes. And he was doing a good job tailgating me.

"Get off my ass," I muttered, brake checking a couple of times in the hopes that he would get the hint. When, the second time, he hit my bumper lightly and didn't make any sort of attempt at stopping, I knew Rosie was right.

This wasn't some idiot tailgating me. This was some idiot trying to run me off the road.

I'd just bought this car. I didn't want to have to get the smell of pee out of the seat right away. I had to keep my cool. Whatever; this was fine. Just some crazy person trying to run us off the road.

"I'm guessing you don't have something super useful in that bag, like a rocket launcher?" I asked Rosie. "Or at the very least a gun?"

Rosie shook her head, glancing at the side mirror. "Sorry. It's going to have to be you versus him. Do you have a plan?"

"Believe it or not, I don't actually spend my whole day imagining what would happen if the person in the car behind me tried to run me off the road. So no, I don't."

"I guess now would be a good time to put my seatbelt on, huh?" Dot asked from the back seat.

"What?" I screeched. "You weren't wearing it before? We were trying not to get pulled over by the cops!"

"I wanted to be able to make a quick getaway if you were pulled over! Besides, it's nighttime. It's not like the cops could *see* if I was wearing one. I'm a woman who looks of an age that would always wear a seatbelt."

Okay, she had a point there.

"Well, put your seatbelt on now, because the cops are about to be the least of our problems," I said.

We reached the intersection with Wailea Alanui Drive, and I turned right, heading back toward Kihei while I tried to figure out the best course of action here.

"Do you have any tips for me?" I asked Rosie.

"Keep your wits about yourself. Deep breaths. That's going to get us all through this. And don't turn that steering wheel too fast; this seems like the kind of car that wants to roll."

That was a good point. I really hoped that didn't happen. I'd had Queenie for less than a day. We were just getting to know each other. I didn't want her trashed immediately.

The speed limit along here was thirty, but with the truck constantly coming up behind me, I found myself pressing the accelerator more and more. There weren't a lot of cars on the road tonight, and with it being a double-lane street there was plenty of space to speed by.

The truck rammed the back of the Jeep again lightly, and I bit my lip in frustration. I had to think of something, and fast.

Then, before I knew it, the headlights disappeared from my rearview. The roar of an engine revving reached my ears, and I looked over to see the truck flying up in the lane next to me.

"I'm getting a picture of him," Dot shouted as I focused on the road in front of us. There was a small Toyota sedan in the lane the truck was in, about two hundred feet ahead.

"All right, Queenie, let's see what you can do," I muttered as I gunned the accelerator right as the truck turned into me.

The horrible screeching sound of metal on metal reached my ears as Queenie started veering toward the curb on the left. Instead of fighting it, I let the car jump the curb with the two left wheels, since fighting it would result in me spinning out. This way, not only was I able to keep Queenie moving forward, but I still had enough of her on the road that the truck would have to stop when it reached the sedan or hit the car and risk damaging his own vehicle so he couldn't keep chasing us.

Of course, the downside to being half on the curb was that the ride had become significantly bumpier. Rosie reached forward and grabbed the dashboard to steady herself, while I began to wonder if this thing had airbags that were about to go off; 1993 was a long time ago, and surely they hadn't been invented back then, right?

The car bobbed up and down as I gunned it forward, and sure enough, as I reached the Toyota sedan, the truck was forced to ease off. He slowed down, giving me the space to get back into the lane and fly by the Toyota as fast as possible before I reached the intersection with Okolani Drive.

"Good work," Rosie said calmly as we approached the four-way intersection.

"We're not done yet," I muttered. The truck's headlights were growing in my rearview pretty quickly. I made to go right, then at the last minute swung the steering wheel hard left. Pain seared through my arm as I was thrown toward Rosie by the forces on me, and the left wheels actually lifted off the ground for a split second before falling back down to earth. The Jeep didn't skip a beat and zoomed up Okolani Drive like it was nothing.

"You can thank me and the McDonald's I had for lunch," Dot said. "That's what got us over the edge on keeping the car on four wheels."

"We're just lucky you weren't on my side of the car. Is he still behind us?"

"Affirmative," Dot said, and I swore as I moved the car even faster. Okay. I had to think. This was my home. Okolani Drive was turning into South Kihei Drive in a moment, an avenue I knew better than almost anywhere else in the world. I had to get away from this guy somehow.

Then it hit me. Once we hit South Kihei Road, the houses on the left all backed onto the beach. There was one in particular that had a huge entrance, with a bunch of cars that always sat empty on the lot. The lot led directly to a thicket of bushes that backed onto the beach. I was really glad I'd gone for the Jeep and not a sensible Corolla.

"All right, hold on," I warned the others as we reached the house in question. I yanked the steering wheel to the left once more, and the tires screeched along the road as I slammed on the brakes. As soon as we were past the gate and on the property, I slammed the gas pedal to the floor once more.

The Jeep immediately responded—Olivia had done some good work to the internal workings of the engine—and darted forward, speeding toward the bushes at the end of the property.

"Here goes nothing," I muttered as the Jeep shot directly into the low-rising bushes. The vehicle jumped and jolted, and I grabbed the exterior frame with my left hand to center myself somewhat. Then, with a final lurch, Queenie shot out of the bushes and onto the sands of Keawakapu beach.

The initial bounce was so hard that my head slammed forward and hit the steering wheel. Pain seared through my head, and my field of vision narrowed, dots flickering in my vision, but I managed to stay conscious. A piece of errant plant material was stuck under one of the windshield wipers and flopping noisily on the glass, but apart from that, the car seemed to have come out of this relatively unscathed, all things considered.

About fifty feet in front of the Jeep, directly in its path, was a couple obviously enjoying a pleasant nighttime stroll on the beach. As soon as the headlights landed on them, they turned around. The woman froze, a horrified expression on her face. Her boyfriend, ever the gentleman, jumped to the side himself. I yanked the steering wheel to the left, and the Jeep missed the woman by inches.

"If you'd hit her, she'd be reincarnated as a deer in her next life," Dot said from the back as I my eyes darted to the rearview mirror for a quick glance.

I swore when the headlights reappeared.

"Seriously?" Dot asked, spinning her head to have a look. "You have got to be kidding me. How did he follow you? You're driving like a nut."

With the tide being low, I steered the Jeep closer to the water, where the sand was water-logged and a little bit easier to drive on. Thankfully, with the sun having gone down, most people had abandoned the beach for the night. I was barely a good enough driver to keep this Jeep on the road, let alone playing slalom with other people.

The truck quickly pulled up next to me once more. I gritted my teeth, looking over at the driver. He wore a balaclava, hiding his features, but grinned at me through the mouth opening. Then he swung the truck to the left.

It took all my strength to keep the Jeep on the

beach instead of ending up in the water. Sparks flew from the collision between the two vehicles.

"Dot, get the camera," Rosie shouted.

A moment later, to my surprise, Rosie reached through the open window of the man's truck and yanked off his mask.

The expression of shock on the man's face would have been glorious to savor, but I didn't have time.

"Kodak moment!" Dot shouted as the camera's flash momentarily blinded me.

He shouted something at Dot and then turned the car away. A moment later, he went to ram us again.

I chose that moment to slam on the brakes.

The seatbelt dug so deeply into my shoulder that I couldn't breathe for a moment, but once again, Olivia's work came through as the Jeep screeched to a halt. The truck sailed directly in front of us before careening directly into the ocean, coming to a stop. The man tried to reverse, but the wheels spun in the sand for a second before the engine flooded, sputtering for a moment before shutting off completely.

I slowed the Jeep down then reversed toward the truck as the man struggled to get out of the car, the water pressing against the door and preventing him from opening it. Eventually, he crawled out the window but tripped on the sill on his way out and landed face-first in the waves below with a splash.

When the man finally reached the shore, spluttering and coughing up a lung—along with what seemed like half the contents of the Pacific Ocean—

he glared at us, water dripping off his body. "What the hell is wrong with you?"

"Hey, you're the one who tried running us off the road."

"Yeah, but you're the crazy bitch who drove onto the beach. Who *does* that?"

"Who are you?" I asked, ignoring his question. "And why did you try to kill us?"

"I don't have to answer to you."

"You do if you don't want me to run you over with my Jeep."

"I'll go back into the water if you try."

"Then you'll drown. Trust me, I'm okay with that outcome too."

The man eyed the three of us and laughed. "You can't be serious. You took two old ladies from a retirement home and drive a car that's almost as old as they are. You really think you're going to do anything to me?"

"I don't know. Your truck seems like it's out of commission, and I bet my Jeep is *really* good at hunting people down if they try and run." I smirked at the guy, and that was when he pulled out a little black box from his pocket that I recognized all too well. "Oh ,shi —" was all I had time to say before the two probes shot out toward me.

Pain seared through my body as every muscle I had contracted, and then everything went black.

Chapter 12

My eyes fluttered open to the rhythmic beeping of a heart rate monitor, alerting me to the fact that my faster-than-normal pace meant I was out of shape, yes, but not quite dead just yet.

"Are you trying to get a frequent-flyer discount?" Zoe's voice said next to me. "Because I'm afraid we don't offer those here."

I groaned and leaned back against the bed as everything came back to me. The car chase. The man with the balaclava. And then the Taser. I opened my left eye and looked at my friend. She was dressed in jeans and a cute tank top with a rainbow across the front, obviously here as Zoe and not as Dr. Morgan. The way she leaned casually back in the chair meant there was very little chance I was about to drop dead from complications due to being Tasered too many times.

"Where are Dot and Rosie?" I managed to ask.

"They brought you in, but they left in a rush.

They're the ones who called me. They asked me to call when you were ready to be discharged—pun very much intended—and said they'd come and pick you up."

"Thanks for coming," I said gratefully.

Zoe smiled, reaching across and squeezing my hand.

I reached over for a glass of water, and she handed it to me.

"Of course. You're my best friend. Besides, I really need you to sign that lease. Your mother asked me tonight if I was a lesbian and if that's why I'm not married with babies yet."

I choked on the water, half of it going down the wrong hole and the other half dribbling down my chin and dropping onto the front of my hospital gown as I tried to cough my airways clear.

Zoe giggled. "Sorry. I probably should have waited for you to swallow."

"There's a Steve Carell–style joke there, but I'm too sore and tired to make it. I'm sorry about Mom. She asked me the same thing the other day, too. You know how guys think with their dicks? Mom thinks with her shriveled-up ovaries, and since I wasn't around, I guess she figured you were as good a target as any."

"Ovaries don't *shrivel.*"

"I know that," I lied. "It's an expression."

"No, it isn't."

"Whatever. Anyway, did you say yes to get her off your back? Because I need to know. She'll figure out you're lying if you told her you're gay but didn't tell me."

Zoe's light laugh rang across the room. "No, I didn't. I told her the truth: I'm a doctor who spends so much time working that I don't have time for a relationship, but hopefully, in a few more years, when I'm a bit more stable, I'll be able to devote the time to find a man."

"Let me guess: she wasn't happy with that."

"She told me she was going to call my boss and explain that it's not right that doctors have to work so hard that pretty young women like myself don't have time to find a husband."

I groaned. "Yeah, that's Mom."

"It's okay," Zoe said, rifling through her purse and coming out with a pen and paper. "But for the love of all that is holy, *please* sign this right now so I can get us the keys to our new place."

I laughed lightly, but pain seared through my side, and I clutched at it for a moment before taking the pen from Zoe and signing where she pointed.

"What were you doing, anyway?" Zoe asked when the papers were signed. "You look like you got into a car accident or something."

"Something like that," I muttered. "Did you know Tasers work after they get wet?"

"I heard that if you get them wet, they can go off without warning," Zoe said with a shrug. "Who did this to you, anyway? You're not under arrest this time, so I assume it wasn't a cop. Why did someone have a wet Taser?"

I blew air out of my cheeks and leaned back against the pillow once more. "If you get me some morphine or something, I'll tell you the whole story." Great. Now I sounded like Dot. But in my defense, I'd just had thousands of volts of electricity shot through my body. I was pretty sure I deserved it.

"Fine. But I swear, if you're getting yourself Tasered regularly so you can get the fun drugs…"

"I'd probably find a much less painful way to manipulate you into it," I interrupted.

"That's true. Okay, I'll be right back. But then you have to spill," Zoe said with a laugh and a wag of her finger in my direction as she got up off the chair and went to get me some morphine. She returned a few minutes later with a couple of pills, which she handed me. I tilted my head back and swallowed the pills with the help of the glass of water. I was pretty sure anybody who could swallow pills dry was secretly a serial killer.

"All right, strap in," I said, shifting around to get comfortable. Well, as comfortable as one can when they feel like they've just been hit by a bus.

"Uh oh. If *you're* the one saying that, I know this story is going to be a ride."

"That it is," I said with a grin.

TEN MINUTES LATER, I'D TOLD ZOE EVERYTHING, and her jaw hung practically down to the floor.

"There are so many parts to that story that are

unbelievable, I don't even know where to start. Where's your car now?"

I sighed. "I have no idea. I just got Queenie too. I guess she's still on the beach. It probably won't take long before the cops find it and trace it back to me. Any chance you can get me discharged? I'd like to have the option of going on the run if I have to."

"You still owe half the rent on our new place if you go to jail," Zoe said with a grin. "You should probably be adding my mom's number to your phone's speed dial, what with her being a lawyer and all, just in case."

"You don't seem especially worried."

"Well, you were being chased. That has 'mitigating circumstances' written all over it."

"I hope you're right," I muttered.

"What happened to the man coming after you, anyway?"

"I have no idea. I guess I'll have to wait for Dot and Rosie to come by and catch me up. Listen, why don't you get some rest? We have a big day ahead of us tomorrow anyway if we're moving. When do you work next?"

"I start my shift in an hour. And it's going to be a long one." Zoe stifled a yawn.

"Are you joking? Go get some coffee. Or some rest. Just don't tell my mom where I am, whatever you do." I said.

"I'm not leaving you alone. You're obviously in constant need of adult supervision."

"Dot and Rosie were with me."

"And apparently they don't qualify as adults."

"You're exhausted. At the very least, go find the staff room and sleep there. Trust me, I'm tired too. And the morphine is starting to kick in. I won't get into any trouble before morning, I promise."

"I'll wait. I'm not leaving you here alone. Besides, you're probably going to be discharged soon anyway. I'll go find your doctor and have a chat with him."

Zoe stood up from the chair and left the room, returning about a minute later. "The doctor will be in to see you in a few minutes. I'm going to call Dot and Rosie; they want to be the ones to pick you up."

I flashed Zoe a grateful smile. "Thanks. Seriously, I'm good from here. Get a bit of rest before your shift. Tomorrow's going to be a big day."

"Are you sure?"

"Yeah. Don't worry. Dot and Rosie will get me home safely."

"I dunno. They didn't seem that great at it last time," Zoe said, one side of her mouth curling upward into a small smile. "But all right. I'll text you tomorrow. Are you working?"

"Yeah, at ten."

"Great. I'm meeting Iris at eight to swap this lease for the keys."

"That's far too early," I chuckled. "But okay, we'll meet sometime around then. I don't really have all that much stuff to move anyway."

"Me either," Zoe admitted with a shrug. "I rented my old place out already furnished, so I've really just got that one box that's at your mom's place."

"That sounds good to me. I love a quick move. Anything we need we can get off Craigslist."

"Exactly what I was thinking. All right, I'll talk to you in the morning."

FIFTEEN MINUTES LATER, AFTER A QUICK confirmation from the doctor that I was going to be fine and was free to go whenever my ride arrived, Dot yanked aside the privacy curtain, rushing in with Rosie hot on her heels.

"We hear you're being set free," Dot said, and I nodded.

"Good. Come on. Don't say anything until we're out of the hospital."

"Where's Queenie? Is she okay? What happened to that guy?"

"What did I *just* say?" Dot asked with an exasperated sigh. "We'll tell you everything. But not here."

Wondering what all the secrecy was about, I gathered my things—which amounted to the top I'd been wearing, which had been removed and replaced with a hospital gown, likely to check that my heart hadn't suffered permanent damage from the Taser—and followed them out of the hospital.

When we reached the parking lot, I squealed when I spotted a familiar blue car in the lot. "Queenie!"

"She's been through it," Dot said, jingling the keys.

Under the warm glow of the streetlight, I did my

best to inspect the damage. Sure enough, the passenger-side door was dented inward, with scrapes and scratches all over the gorgeous paint. The side mirror had come off at some point—I wasn't entirely sure what it said about my skill as a driver that I hadn't noticed, but it probably wasn't good—and the windshield had been chipped, but apart from that, she looked in remarkably good shape.

"Well, I guess I'm going to see just how good a mechanic Olivia is," I said with a chuckle as I got into the passenger seat. Rosie hopped into the driver's side while Dot took the back. "Now can I ask what happened after I passed out? Are we all going to be arrested?"

"I doubt it," Dot said. "Although I wouldn't rule anything out just yet."

"Who was the guy who chased us? Do you know? Did he get away?"

"That's the thing about your generation, you're always in such a rush," Dot said. "Don't worry. You'll find out everything in due time."

I rolled my eyes. "Gee, sorry for wanting to know what happened to the guy who Tasered me."

Rosie grinned. "Let's just say he probably won't be Tasering anyone anytime soon."

"Oh my God, you didn't kill him, did you? And if you did, is the body well hidden? Of course it would be. What am I saying? But seriously, is he dead?"

"Not yet," Dot said ominously.

"Okay, now I'm *really* curious."

We pulled up to Dot's building, and as soon as she

opened the door to the apartment, she quickly ushered Rosie and me through the frame and shut the door behind us. I understood why immediately when the muffled sounds of someone being held against their will reached my ears.

"You *kidnapped* him?" I hissed.

"What else did you want us to do? He didn't leave us a choice. Besides, it's fine. I had this apartment soundproofed years ago. As long as that front door stays closed, we can do whatever we want to him, and no one will ever be the wiser."

"I know that was meant to be reassuring, but somehow, it's really not."

Who knew that possession of enough drugs to tranquilize a herd of elephants was going to be one of the lesser crimes I committed tonight?

Chapter 13

I headed down the hall, following the thumps and moans, until I reached the bathroom. I swung the door open to find the man who had Tasered me lying in the bathtub. His mouth had been sealed shut with duct tape featuring a Hello Kitty design on the front. The rest of the roll sat on the bathroom counter next to a pair of scissors. The man's hands were zip-tied in front of him, as were his feet and legs at his ankles and knees.

His eyes widened when he saw me, and he began moaning with more energy, moving around the bathtub but sliding around like a wet cat, unable to get purchase on the slippery surface.

"Oh, shut up," Dot said to him, passing in front of me and standing over the man. "Are you going to be quiet if I take the tape off? Because this place is soundproof. No one can hear you scream if you try, and it's just going to annoy me. Got it?"

The man nodded, and Dot reached down, ripping the tape from his mouth with a single quick movement. I winced as the ripping sound rang across the room.

"These bitches are crazy," he said to me, desperation in his eyes. "You see what they've done? They've kidnapped me! You have to save me."

I laughed. "Sorry, I make it a rule not to help people who have Tasered me in the last twelve hours. Maybe you should have thought of that first."

"Look, I'm sorry about that. I didn't mean to. It just went off."

"Yeah, sure. You sound like the kind of guy who sends dick pics to women on Tinder and then pretends it was an accident when they call him out on it."

"No! No, it's nothing like that. Look, there's obviously been some mistake. I don't want to hurt you."

"Well, your actions said differently. But don't worry, I'm willing to look past that if you tell us what we want to know." I looked at Dot and Rosie. "Have you questioned him yet?"

"No, we figured it would be best to let him stew for a little while and think about what he'd done," Rosie replied with a small smile. "And to think about what we could do to him."

"You're crazy! Are you going to kill me?"

The slightest waver in the man's voice at the end of the last question betrayed the fact that he was absolutely terrified. And so he should have been.

"Not if you tell us what we need to know."

"Fine. Fine, I'll tell you anything. Just let me go

after. I promise I won't go to the cops. I'm sorry for the whole Taser thing. It was an accident. I won't ever do it again."

I grinned. I was pretty sure this guy would pee himself on cue if I asked him to right now. "All right, why did you come after us? Who sent you?"

"You were looking for Jo's stash. I needed to know if you found it."

"You mean the drugs."

The man nodded.

"All right. What's your name?"

"Phil."

"Come on, Phil what?"

"McCracken."

"Okay, what's your *real* name?"

The man scowled. "That *is* my real name."

"I don't believe you. There's no way you're actually called Phil McCracken."

The man's eyes dropped to his pants. "My wallet's in my back pocket. You're welcome to check it if you don't believe me."

"I'll take your word for it for now. All right, Phil McCracken. So you were after Jo's stash."

"Yeah. Just because she's dead doesn't mean I'm going to leave her product. Bitch already owed me twenty Gs. I can't afford to lose that much. At the very least, I was going to get my stuff back."

"So, you were her dealer," Dot said.

Phil's eyes moved to her. "Duh. How do you fit in? Did you buy her greenies?"

"Greenies?" I asked.

"Street slang for Percocet," Dot explained.

"How do you know that and I don't?" I muttered to myself as Dot answered Phil.

"We're trying to find who killed her. And right now, we really like you for it. So unless you want to see your ass dumped in front of the police station when we're done, why don't you tell us everything you know about Jo and her death?"

"Whoa, whoa," Phil said, flailing about in the tub a little bit more. "I don't know anything about her death. Seriously. I heard she got herself killed, but that had nothing to do with me."

"Help us believe you," I said, plastering the falsest smile I could on my face and resting my hand on my chin.

"Okay, look. Here's the thing. Jo and I went to high school together. That's how I know her. Knew her. We kept in touch, and she found out I was dealing. She wanted in."

"Why?" Rosie asked. "She was loaded."

"Yeah, and she hated the pressure her dad put on her. She wasn't in it for the money. She wanted to rebel. She wanted to be cool. She wanted to do something her parents would disapprove of. And hey, it made me some cash, so what do I care?"

"When did this start?"

"When she was in college. She'd sneak the pills on the plane. She was a rich white girl; no one was going to look too closely at her stuff. She'd take the drugs with her then pay me when she came back. I figured when she graduated, she'd be done with the stuff, but she kept doing it."

"Was she sampling the merchandise?" Rosie asked.

"If she was, she was paying for it. At least at first."

"Yeah, you said she owed you twenty grand?" I asked.

Phil nodded. "She swore she was good for it. Said she just got behind a bit. And I mean, given who her family is, I figured she was telling the truth. If it came to it, the old man would rather pay up than see her show up to Sunday dinner with a pair of busted kneecaps, you know?"

"How does someone like Jo Lismore get behind on paying you for her drugs? She had a good-paying job, and she was rich as anything."

"I'm pretty sure Tommy had something to do with it. That's why she dumped him. She didn't actually come out and say it, but I could read between the lines."

Phil McCracken didn't look like he could read anything, let alone between the lines, but I let it slide. "So if you didn't kill her, who do you think did?"

"Beats me. How would I know?"

"Seeing as you're her supplier and she owed you twenty grand, that would make you suspect numero uno if you don't come up with something better, genius. So, do you want to help yourself out here a bit?"

Phil let out an annoyed huff. "Fine. I don't like that

boyfriend of hers. Tommy. He lost his meal ticket and was publicly humiliated when she broke up with him to boot."

"Oh?"

Phil grinned for the first time since arriving. "Yeah. It was beautiful from what I saw. They were at the Alaloa Lounge, celebrating Jo's birthday. She had a dozen of her friends there, all dressed to the nines. Then halfway through the night, they start arguing, because Tommy told the waitress the hottest thing in the restaurant wasn't on the menu."

"Ugh," I said, rolling my eyes.

"Anyway, Jo got pissed. They start fighting, right there. She dumped her hurricane over him, and he tried to punch her in the face. She managed to avoid the hit, kicked him in the balls, and two of her male friends dumped him over the railing of the lanai and onto the bushes under it. Word is security escorted him off the premises."

My mouth dropped open. "Wow."

"Yeah." Phil grinned. "I saw some of it; one of Jo's friends Snapchatted it to me. Management politely asked Jo's party to pack it up after that."

"Well, it's the Ritz-Carlton, no kidding."

"Of course, Jo's birthday was already ruined by then. She was sobbing, she had friends trying to make her feel better, and I hear they packed her up in a cab."

"And that's when she and Tommy broke up?"

"She hasn't taken his calls since from what she told me. He's been calling her too. She showed me her phone once; she had twenty missed calls from him. Dude was desperate. Desperate enough to kill her? I dunno. I could for sure see him getting annoyed and accidentally offing her."

"Anyone else?"

Phil shrugged. "Nah. Not that I know of, anyway. Look, it's not like we were best buds or anything. We have some mutual friends, but our relationship was mostly business. I don't know what else was going on in her life. But I'm telling you, I didn't kill her. Why would I? There's no way I'm getting my cash now. Or the pills she had in supply to sell. I guess the cops found them."

"Are you the one who broke into Jo's place to search it?" Rosie asked.

"Fine. Yeah, I am. As soon as the cops left, I went in and had a look, but I couldn't find her stash. I figured either the cops had gotten to it, or I missed it. Then I spotted you guys coming in as I was leaving, and I figured I'd see if you'd found the pills. Did you?" Phil looked from one face to the other for an answer.

Dot grinned. "You should have looked at her tampons."

Phil made a face. "Gross."

"And that reaction right there is exactly why that's where she hid them," Dot said with a satisfied smirk. "Men. You all pretend to be so tough, but you're scared of a little blood,"

"Look, that stuff's disgusting, okay? Now, I've told you everything I know. Are you going to let me out of here?"

"What do you think?" Dot asked, turning to Rosie and me. "Should we let him go? Or should we add his head to our collection of skulls?"

I don't think I've ever seen a man's face go so white so quickly.

Chapter 14

It wasn't like we had any proof that Phil McCracken was a drug dealer, after all. We could have dropped him off at the police station, but what good would that have done?

Instead, we decided to drop him off at an unknown location. Dot and Rosie would take care of that, and I could drive home with the pills, which I'd give to Zoe in the morning to test.

Dot dragged an enormous suitcase that reached nearly up to her hips from the living room, and I eyed it carefully. "Are you sure you two are going to be fine getting him into Rosie's car in that?" I asked.

"Of course we are," Dot said. "We got him up here, didn't we?"

That was a fair point.

"Look at it this way: the last guy who underestimated us because we're old is now lying zip-tied in the bathtub," Rosie added.

That was an even better point.

"All right, well, in the interest of being able to count all the felonies I've committed tonight on only two hands, I'm going to get going," I said. "I'll text you tomorrow. Are you going to bother running those prints now that we know they're Phil's?"

"Might as well have a look," Dot said with a shrug. "You never know."

"Good call. Okay, thanks for the help tonight."

"Try not to get Tasered on your way home," Dot said with a grin.

I was too tired to come up with a pithy reply, so I flipped her the bird and headed back down to Queenie.

I also had to call Olivia and see if she could do wonders to my brand-new ride, which looked like it had come out of a bad *Jurassic Park* adventure.

BY THE TIME I GOT HOME, IT WAS NEARLY TWO IN the morning. Mom was asleep on the couch; she had obviously tried to stay up to make sure I'd gotten home safely. A creepy looking man on the TV with no shirt and way too much oil on his chest proclaimed the benefits of some sort of weight-loss powder. *For only three easy payments of $19.99, you too can look like a smiley fry that was left in the oil for a few seconds too long.*

Did anyone ever actually buy this crap?

I grabbed the remote and turned off the TV, the sound of it causing Mom to stir. I placed a blanket on top of her.

"Charlie?"

"It's okay, Mom. Go to sleep.

"I'm glad you're home safe."

"Me too, Mom. Don't worry about me."

Mom muttered something else under her breath but was obviously halfway back to dreamland, so I tiptoed out of the room and collapsed onto my own bed, wishing I could crawl under the covers and sleep for about thirty hours.

Unfortunately, it felt like only thirty seconds passed before my alarm blared me back to reality. I slapped my hand around on the nightstand until I found the phone then groaned as I turned off the alarm.

Every inch of my body was sore, and I wasn't sure if it was the sleep deprivation or the thousands of volts of electricity that had coursed through my body earlier that had caused it.

It was probably a bit of column A and a bit of column B if I was honest about it.

As I threw on whatever half-clean clothes I managed to find on the floor, I started wondering what was the biggest coffee Starbucks could make me, and in a half-functional daze, I managed to make it to the car and drive to the closest drive-through.

It was just after eight when I pulled up to the apartment building, a trenta vanilla sweet-cream cold brew sitting in the cup holder. That's right, this was a thirty-ounces-of-coffee kind of day. But it was all worth it to see the apartment. My new apartment.

I parked in a visitor's spot—I didn't know which ones were the two spots for Zoe and me—and looked up at the building for a moment before I heard Zoe's voice.

"Well, if I thought you were kidding when you told me that story last night, one look at this car would set me straight."

I turned and scrunched up my face. "It's that bad, huh?"

"It's that bad," Zoe confirmed. "But hey, as long as she still drives, that's the important thing."

"I'll get Olivia to fix her up," I said, stepping out of the car and giving Zoe a quick hug.

"Good plan. You're getting your expenses covered, right?"

I nodded.

She handed me a set of keys. "These are yours, dear roommate."

"You have no idea how happy it makes me to hear you say that," I said. "I love my mom, but she's... a lot."

Zoe laughed. "That she is. Now, I assume you have your entire life packed into a single suitcase?"

I nodded. "Sure do. Coco is still at Mom's place too. I figured we should settle in and move everything we've got before bringing her over. Otherwise, she's just going to get beneath our feet to see if there's some sort of magic treat machine in every box we move."

"That's probably the right call. Anyway, I don't have much. Just a few boxes. You don't even have to help. It's all my stuff, so if you want to just settle in, I can bring it up."

"Are you kidding?" I said with a snort. "Of course I'm going to help you."

Between the two of us, it took less than ten minutes to take all the boxes upstairs, and that was including three separate pee breaks for me. The coffee might have been a mistake.

"I took the liberty of ordering a couple of mattresses and a couch, since I kind of assumed you weren't going to do it," Zoe said.

"You assumed correctly," I replied. "Thanks. Let me know how much I owe you."

Zoe waved a hand. "Don't worry about it. Consider it a thanks for saving me from that creep."

"You're the best. I'm buying you dinner when you next get a day off. And we're going somewhere fancy. With tablecloths."

"Deal. You're working today, right? I can stay here and wait for the delivery drivers."

I nodded. "My shift starts at ten."

"And given how much coffee you've already drunk, I'm going to go ahead and assume you didn't get much sleep last night."

"That would be a fair assumption."

"What happened with the man who Tasered you?"

"Dot and Rosie overpowered him, kidnapped him, took him to Dot's apartment, where we questioned him, and then dragged him back to their car in a suit-case. I assume they set him free, but to be honest, I'm not entirely sure. Oh, and the best part of it all is his name was Phil McCracken."

Zoe raised an eyebrow. "Sometimes I wonder if you make things up just to see how I'll react."

"Oh, trust me, none of this is made up. And while I'm on the subject, I need a favor," I added, rushing over to the kitchen island—this apartment had an *island*!—where I'd set down my purse earlier. I dug through it until I found the box of Tampax and the Advil.

I held them up.

"That time of the month?"

"What? No, look inside."

I tossed Zoe the bottle of Advil, and she popped the lid, pouring a couple of pills into her hand.

"Well, that'll certainly kill your period pain."

"Can you find out for me if it's real?"

"The pills? Yeah, I can do that. I assume they're related to Jo's death?"

"I'm not completely sure, but it's an avenue to explore. She was dealing for Phil McCracken."

"His parents had to realize how stupid a name that was when he was born, right?"

"You would think so."

Zoe shook her head. "Some people. Anyway, yes, I can test it for you. Although given the quantity you seem to have there, I might just grab a sampling of pills. What are you going to do with the rest of them?"

I shrugged. "Honestly, I'm not sure yet. Maybe I'll give them to the cops. They were probably looking for them when they searched her apartment. A part of me feels like if they weren't willing to look in the tampon box, they probably don't deserve to have them, but then at the same time, if it helps them find a killer, it's probably the right thing to do to hand them over, right?"

A smile flittered on Zoe's lips. "Yes, giving the police evidence to potentially help them find a killer *is* the right thing to do, no matter how much you think they do or don't deserve it. I might not be the biggest fan of the police, but you should probably hand it over."

"Okay. It's not like I'm going to keep it. Although given the way I feel right now, I'm tempted to pop a couple of them just to dull the pain a bit."

"Absolutely not," Zoe said. "You have a tendency to make questionable life choices at the best of times, but I draw the line at taking random pills that you found in a murder victim's bathroom."

"They look like Percocet," I said with a shrug.

"How you made it this far without accidentally poisoning yourself will always be a mystery to me. If you really need some drugs to get over your pain, *please* ask your roommate and best friend to write you a prescription rather than taking random pills just because they *look* like Percocet."

"Fine. I think I'll be okay, though."

"Good. If not, let me know. I mean it, I don't want you taking this stuff until I've had it tested to see what it's made of. There's a lot of crap in street drugs these days."

"Thanks. I appreciate the help."

"Of course. Frankly, what you've said about Jo seems pretty sad."

I nodded. "Yeah. That's the impression I'm getting too. It sounds like she really wanted to get out of the shadow of her family, especially her dad, but just didn't quite know how to do it. Anyway, I have to get going. My shift starts soon."

"I'll see you later. I'm going to pick up some stuff we're going to need, like dishes. Do you care what I buy?"

"We both know that not only do I not care, but you care way too much and won't want to buy what I like anyway."

"Great," Zoe said. "I'm glad we're in agreement. Have fun at work. Are you feeling ok this morning?"

"I mean, all things considered? Yeah. I could use a twelve-hour nap, but I'll survive."

I gave her a quick wave and grabbed my purse from the counter as I left the apartment. I was halfway down the hall leading to the stairs when the door to an apartment on my left opened. I smiled, looking forward to meeting my new neighbor, but when my eyes landed on a familiar face, I stopped dead in my tracks.

Jake stared at me for a moment, stepped back into his apartment, and closed the door. When he reopened it a minute later, he shook his head. "And here I was hoping I'd just imagined you standing here in front of me. Please tell me you're just visiting someone."

"I've made a huge mistake," I whispered.

Chapter 15

"Tell me you don't live here," I said.

"Yeah, I live here," Jake replied. "Please tell me *you're* not the one who just moved in down the hall."

"I am. Zoe knows the landlord through work. Obviously, this means you're going to have to move."

"What? I lived here first. *You're* going to have to move. Tell the landlord you've changed your mind. I don't want to live near your crazy ass."

"How do you think I feel?"

"Like you're living in a secure building because there's a police officer down the hall?"

I snorted. "Please. There are safer war zones out there than living next to you and your humpty-dumpty partner. You're more Keystone Cops than Hawaii Five-0 as far as I'm concerned."

The corner of Jake's mouth curled upward. "You're eventually going to have to let that go."

"Yeah, I'm a big fan of glossing over police brutality."

Jake rubbed his face with his hands. "I can't believe this is happening. You can't be my neighbor. Although actually, this suddenly makes a lot of sense. Is that your Jeep in the visitor's lot?"

"So what if it is?"

"Well, someone reported a neon-blue jeep being chased down the beach by a Toyota Tacoma last night. When officers got there, the Tacoma was found floating in the ocean, but there was no sign of the Jeep."

"Huh. It must have been someone else's car."

"Right, because there are two neon-blue Wranglers from the early nineties driving around this island."

"How long have you lived here? I bet there's at least five of them."

Jake scowled at me. "Does this have to do with the fact that you're investigating Jo Lismore's murder for her father? Because we need to have a chat about that too."

"Yeah, I've heard you're not going to give me anything that might help with the investigation."

"That's because you're not a cop," Jake growled. "You're not even a licensed private investigator. I don't know who's the dumber one of the two of you: the guy who hired an ice cream scooper to investigate his daughter's murder or the ice cream scooper who actually said yes."

"If you're so good at solving murders, how come I

was the one who figured out who killed James MacMahon? Especially since I'm *just* an ice cream scooper. That must be really embarrassing for you."

"We were going to get there. But we have to gather evidence instead of going around half-cocked after murderers. I'll remind you that you almost ended up dead."

"'Almost' being the key word in that sentence."

"No, 'dead' was *obviously* the key word there. You're unbelievable. You don't have any training in this sort of thing. Believe it or not, I don't want your murder to be the next one I have to investigate."

"And you're not going to have to."

"That's funny, because from the reports I got last night, it sure sounded like it was close."

"I'm standing right here in front of you though, aren't I?"

"So, you admit it was you driving the Jeep that was chased down by the Tacoma."

"I said nothing of the sort."

"Do we really have to do this? We both know it was you. What happened to the driver of the Tacoma? Is he okay, at least, or do we need to send divers into the water?"

"If I knew you needed to do that, I would tell you, because *I'm* happy to share information," I replied. I wasn't about to admit to Jake that my Jeep had in fact been the one he was after, but I also wasn't going to send him on a wild goose chase for a body that didn't exist. I hoped.

Jake ran a hand through his hair, and I tried not to

think about just how good it looked when it had been freshly tousled and how much I wanted to run my hands through those locks too. And all over other parts of him.

Infuriating and sexy was the worst combination.

"You're really not going to admit it was you, then?"

"No, of course I'm not."

"And I suppose it's pointless for me to tell you to stay away from my case?"

"I've got a job to do," I replied with a shrug.

"It's not your job. Your job is to serve ice cream to tourists and locals on a hot day. That's a nice, safe job. Why can't you keep doing that?"

"This one pays more. Besides, someone tried robbing the store the other day. It's not like it's this bastion of safety you make it out to be."

"A guy who's so drunk he peed himself in the cells is a little bit different to a stone-cold killer who shot a woman with a .38 and dumped her in the ocean."

I grinned. "Thanks for the heads-up on the cause of death."

Jake narrowed his eyes at me. "I'm serious. You're not even a private investigator. You're going to get yourself killed. Stay out of my case, and if I see you interfering, I'm going to arrest you for obstruction of justice. And trust me, the handcuffs aren't going to be nearly as sexy as your mom thinks they are."

My cheeks flushed crimson in a combination of embarrassment and righteous anger. "You leave my mom's weird lack of boundaries out of this. I don't need to get in your way. I'm getting plenty of information on my own, thank you very much. I bet you haven't even spoken to her supplier yet."

"Her supplier?" Jake asked, tilting his head to the side slightly.

A small smile crept across my face. "You don't even know about her drug dealing, do you?"

Jake's face immediately hardened. "I'm not going to talk to you about an open police investigation."

"Right. This totally isn't that you didn't realize she was dealing drugs and are still trying to look like you know what you're doing, because your whole shtick of telling me I'm not a professional and I'm not trained for this comes off a bit hollow when it turns out I know more about the victim's life than you do."

"I don't have time for this. I need to get to work." Jake stepped out into the hall, pulling the door closed. "Stay out of my investigation, Charlie. I won't tell you again."

With that, Jake strode off down the hall, and I watched him, my eyes focusing on his rear end.

"He's a looker, that one," a voice said from behind me, and I jumped nearly a foot in the air. "If I was ten years younger, I'd be all over that."

I turned to find myself looking at a short woman, a couple inches over five feet tall, with wavy, sun-kissed blondish hair and blue eyes that twinkled mischievously. Her tanned skin betrayed that she spent a good chunk of her life outside. I guessed she must have been in her early to mid-forties.

"Sure, if you're into cops who refuse to admit

when they're wrong and get annoyed when you're trying to do your job."

The woman cackled. "Honey, the secret to the hot ones is you can't talk to them. It's the same with athletes. They're too dumb. Just hop on and enjoy the ride… and I mean that literally."

I laughed, holding out a hand. "I'm Charlie. I just moved in down the hall with my best friend, Zoe. We're in number 24."

"Jesper. My apartment's just there, right across from Officer Sexy."

"Lucky you," I said sarcastically.

"There are worse things in life. As I said, I like to admire from afar." Jesper took a step, and I heard a clunk. I looked down to notice her lower left leg was a prosthetic. My eyes widened.

"Shark attack," Jesper said as if it was the most natural thing in the world. "About fifteen years ago, when I was an internationally ranked surfer. He thought I was a seal who would have made a nice snack. Well, he got his snack, all right, but he didn't count on the seal punching him in the nose. Or grabbing onto him as he swam off."

"Did you really?" I asked.

Jesper nodded. "The damn thing swam back under the water, trying to get away from me. I held onto it. I wanted my leg back. You know, it had been with me for twenty-three years at that point. I was quite attached to it. And it had been attached to me, at least until that morning. I wasn't about to let it go without a fight."

"What happened? I'm guessing the shark won?"

"The shark won," Jesper admitted with a shrug. "What can you do? The ocean is their territory; they're at an advantage. But I gave it my best shot. And now I've got Leggy here to replace it. It's not quite the same though. They say you never forget your first love. It turns out the same is true about your first leg."

I let out a snort. "I'll keep that in mind. Anyway, I'm already running behind, so I'm going to let you go before my boss fires me for being late."

"Aloha Ice Cream, huh?" Jesper said, her eyes moving down to the logo in the corner of the shirt I was wearing. "Say hi to Leslie for me."

"I will," I said with a smile. "It was nice meeting you."

"You too."

And with that, I headed down to the parking lot, where Queenie was waiting for me, still in one piece. Mostly, anyway.

I PARKED A FEW BLOCKS AWAY FROM WORK, AND AS I walked over to Aloha Ice Cream, I called Olivia. "Hey, so I had a bit of an adventure with the car yesterday, and I'm wondering if you can fix her up for me," I said when she answered.

Olivia laughed. "What kind of adventure?"

"A drug dealer tried to run me off the road. She's missing a side mirror, and there are a few dents and scratches. Oh, and the windshield is cracked. But apart from that, she's as good as new."

"Well, that all sounds easy enough. Do you want to drop her off at my garage? Or I can come pick her up if you're in Kihei."

"A pickup would be great," I said. "I work at Aloha Ice Cream. You're welcome to come grab the keys whenever, and I'll give you a free cone for the trouble."

"Will do. I'll be there in about an hour."

I thanked Olivia again and hung up the phone. At least Queenie was going to be taken care of, and thanks to Randall paying my expenses, I wasn't even going to be out of pocket.

"Morning," Leslie greeted me with a smile when I walked through the front door a moment later. "How's it going?"

"Good, thanks," I replied. "How's business?"

"A little slow today, but what can you do? It's the middle of the week during shoulder season. I'm not expecting a crowd."

"Hey, I moved this morning and met a woman named Jesper. She told me to say hi."

Leslie grinned. "You're her neighbor?"

I nodded.

"Well, you're in for a treat with that one. Jesper is hilarious, but she's a little crazy. Also, she has a tendency to over exaggerate her stories a little."

"So, she didn't really punch a shark in the nose and ride it through the water to try and get her leg back?" I asked with a small smile.

Leslie chuckled. "Is that what she told you? No. Well, not entirely. She did punch the shark in the nose, but it just looked stunned for a second before swimming off with her leg, and then of course the priority became getting Jesper to the hospital before she bled to death."

"Wait, you were there?"

"Sure. Jesper and I go surfing together all the time. She's much better at it than I am, though."

"You're talking in present tense. She still surfs? Even after losing her leg?"

Leslie grinned. "Jesper is a character in every way. Surfing is her life. She even qualified for some WSL competitions back in the day, back when it was still called ASP. Just because she's down a leg doesn't mean she's going to give up her favorite thing in the world. She still surfs. Her prosthetic is waterproof, and she makes sure to wash it off really well afterward so the salt doesn't mess with it."

"Wow. That's pretty cool," I said.

"That's Jesper in a nutshell. But don't believe everything she tells you. She lives for hyperbole. She's a lot of fun, though."

"Good to know."

I was certainly more enthusiastic about Jesper being my neighbor than Jake.

Chapter 16

L eslie had been right when she said it was a slow day at the ice cream shop. It didn't help that the clouds had rolled in. Of course, this was Maui, and I was pretty sure that at this time of year, we got approximately zero days of rain. But big, white, fluffy clouds in the sky still made ice cream a little less palatable than days when you could cook in the sun without even trying.

When two o'clock rolled around and I could still count on both hands the number of customers I'd served that day, Leslie suggested I head home early. I was all too pleased to take her up on the offer, since I still had a ton of work to do on Jo's murder.

I was going to hunt down Sean Sherman and see if he was the killer.

Of course, the fact that Olivia had taken my car was possibly going to be a problem. I pulled out my phone and called Dot.

"Well, it's good to see you're not in jail," I said when she answered on the second ring.

"I'm too sexy for jail," Dot replied. "What's going on?"

"Did you end up getting an address on Sean Sherman for me?"

"Sure."

"Want to go pay him a visit? Queenie is in the shop getting put back together, so I need a ride."

"Seeing as the alternative involves going to the hairdresser, where Frances Doherty will undoubtedly be going on about her bowel movements and how her fiber-rich cereal has impacted them, I would love nothing more than to drive you. I'll call Frances and let her know something's come up. Pick you up from the front of the store in ten minutes."

Eight minutes later, Dot pulled up with Rosie in front of Aloha Ice Cream, and I hopped into the back seat.

Sean Sherman lived in a low-rise, wood-clad apartment building in Happy Valley, one of the less desirable parts of the island. The painted sign on the side of the building with the street number was peeling so badly it was practically illegible, and the asphalt in the parking lot was cracked and stained with old oil spills. The landscaping was nonexistent, and a dumpster at the far end overflowed. Dot parked the car, and I exited, scrunching up my nose as the smell of garbage reached my nostrils despite our being parked at least forty feet from the dumpster.

There was no shared interior to this building; the

doors on both floors led directly outside, and it didn't take us long to find number 5, Sean Sherman's address. It was one of the ground-floor apartments, and I knocked on the door and waited for an answer.

"Think he's home?" I asked the others.

I was met with a shrug from Rosie and a frown from Dot. "He could also be avoiding us. If he's the killer, he probably doesn't want to speak to anybody," Dot said.

I knocked again, my rap firmer and quicker this time. Another fifteen seconds passed, and there was still no sign of life.

I headed over to the nearby window. The cheap plastic blinds were drawn, but thanks to a broken slat, I was able to peer into the apartment all the same. I couldn't see all that much, but I could make out one thing: a man lying on the living room floor, motionless.

"Uh, I think he might be dead," I said.

Rosie practically shoved me out of the way to get a look herself. "Okay, we're going in," she announced. Pulling out a set of tools from her purse, she made quick work of the front door.

"Yup, that's a totally normal thing to just carry around," I said.

"Well, if he's still alive, it might just save his life," Rosie replied. "Besides, some habits die hard."

I didn't have time to think about whether Rosie was serious, and she'd been wandering around Maui with a set of break-in tools regularly since the sixties. Latex gloves were one thing; robbery tools were another entirely. But hey, who was I to complain when they came in this handy?

The door opened and the three of us piled inside, immediately heading toward where Sherman's body lay.

Rosie darted forward and checked for a pulse. "He's got a pulse, but it's faint."

"We need to call an ambulance," I said.

"No time. Help me carry him to the car. Dot, drive him to the hospital. Charlie, help me search his place before the police get wind of what happened."

The three of us sprang into action. I ran to the other side of the coffee table and grabbed Sean's legs, while Rosie and Dot each grabbed beneath one of his arms.

"One, two, three," Rosie counted, and we hoisted him.

Luckily, Sean was built pretty slim. He couldn't have weighed more than a hundred and sixty pounds, and between us, we were easily able to carry him out the door and back to the car. Rosie even managed to open one of the rear doors without dropping him.

"Are you sure he's not dead?" I asked as we managed to get him fully inside the car. He hadn't moved a muscle or made any kind of noise since we'd carried him from his apartment.

"Not just yet, but he's on his way," Rosie said. "Off you go, Dot. Time to put that lead foot of yours to good use."

Rosie and I stepped out of the way while Dot booked it out of there, tires screeching as she took a left back down toward Main Street. Luckily for Sean, the hospital was only about half a mile away. Rosie had been right; this would be much faster than waiting for an ambulance. I just hoped we weren't too late.

"Come on," Rosie said, pulling me from my thoughts, and the two of us headed right back into Sean's apartment.

The fact that not so much as a single blind had been pulled up to check out the commotion outside was a testament to the part of town we were in. Hopefully, nobody had called the cops, as not only would Rosie and I have a lot of explaining to do, but I wanted to have a good look in Sean's apartment in case he didn't make it.

I was all too aware that this might be the only chance to find evidence he'd killed Jo Lismore. Although as Rosie said she'd felt a pulse, I wasn't exactly confident in Sean Sherman's long-term survival odds.

On the coffee table was a joint as well as a handful of pills scattered around. Tidiness obviously wasn't a priority for Sean; next to the joint were a couple fun-size candy bar wrappers. Someone had gotten the munchies.

Rosie handed me a pair of gloves and I slipped them on. "You wouldn't happen to have some Ziploc bags around, would you?" I asked.

Rosie shook her head. "Sorry, no."

Luckily, dime bags abounded in this apartment, and I quickly found a couple empties sitting on top of the TV cabinet. I put a couple of the pills on the coffee table in one of them. "These look to be the same as the pills we found at Jo's apartment. I'm going to get Zoe to test these as well."

"Good call," Rosie said. "It wouldn't surprise me given what we know about Jo being Sean's dealer."

"Or at least one of them," I said, motioning toward a small pile of off-white powder on the corner of the coffee table. "What do you think that is? Heroin?"

"That would be my best guess," Rosie said, putting on her glasses to get a better look. "I'm not an expert on drugs, though. Collect a sample of that as well and give it to Zoe to test."

"Will do," I said, using a credit card to scrape a sample of the powder into another dime bag. I carefully slipped them both into the back pocket of my jeans. Once again, I really hoped I wasn't going to be arrested anytime soon. I really hadn't expected to be carrying this many drugs around with me while investigating this case.

"You're going to have to learn all of these things if you're going to make more of a career of investigation, you know," Rosie said.

"A career? That wasn't the plan."

"Wasn't it?" Rosie asked, giving me an askance look with a twinkle in her eye. "Because from where I'm sitting, you certainly seem enthusiastic about it."

"I mean, it has it's positives. The money is good. In fact, that's the main positive. The money is amazing. But I wasn't really expecting there to be as many car chases or as much drug dealing as I've ended up with."

Rosie snorted. "That kind of excitement is the best part."

"Well, for those of us who weren't KGB agents sent here to act as sleepers, it's a little bit to get used to."

"I think you should consider getting your investigator's license and doing this sort of thing full-time. You've got some natural instincts."

"Yeah, like I almost instinctively peed myself when Phil hit us with his car."

"Maybe you did. But you also managed to keep the car on the road, you thought of an escape route, and in the end, your car is still functional, while his had to be pulled out from the ocean. The instincts are there. Sure, you're a little bit more like a hippo sloshing through the water than an elegant swan, but at least you're not drowning."

I considered Rosie's words. *Could* this be the kind of thing I could do full-time? No, that was ridiculous. Not a chance.

Before I had the opportunity to think it all through, however, Rosie stood up from behind the couch with a triumphant "Aha!"

I turned to see her triumphantly raising a gun, letting it hang off her index finger, which was slipped through the metal bit that went around the trigger. The gun was silver and relatively new looking. I had to admit, I didn't really know anything about guns. It was one of those little ones with a short barrel at the end, the kind you could easily slip into a purse if you wanted to be armed but subtle about it.

"Please tell me that's a .38," I said.

Rosie grinned. "I might not know much about drugs, but I *do* know guns. This is a Colt Cobra .38 Special. Now, this particular model has a rich history behind it. Jack Ruby used one to kill Lee Harvey Oswald, and Monika Ertl used one to kill the man who cut the hands off Ché Guevara's corpse. Phil Spector also used one to kill Lana Clarkson. Colt stopped making the Cobra in 1981, but in 2017, they began producing it again, and this is a newer model. You can tell not only from the condition of the gun, but the enlarged trigger guard and re-engineered frame are a dead giveaway."

"Well, I didn't understand half those words, but I *did* understand .38 Special, which means that's the same caliber gun as the one used to kill Jo Lismore."

"And that's the most important thing."

"So, wait... does this mean Sean Sherman killed Jo?"

A small smile curled in the corner of Rosie's mouth. "What do you think? You're the investigator."

"I think you're probably much better at this than me. But since you asked... I don't know. I guess I just wasn't expecting it to be this easy."

"You thought it would be more like the movies, where you have to investigate for longer, hunt down some red herrings, that sort of thing?"

I shrugged. "I guess so, yeah. But of course, real life isn't always like that, I guess. Sometimes it really is as easy as finding the murder weapon the junkie used shoved behind the couch at his apartment."

Rosie nodded. "If you hear hooves, look for horses and not zebras. Unless you're in Africa."

"Or the zoo."

Rosie laughed. "Of course, we don't *know* this is the murder weapon, but I think it's a pretty fair assumption to make."

"I'm guessing you don't have some sort of home-made ballistics setup at home so we can test it out?"

"I don't, no, but I also don't have access to the bullet that killed Jo in the first place. The ballistics test is going to be up to the cops."

I sighed. "And let me guess: we're going to have to call them."

"Unless you want to leave this place the way we found it and wait for them to get here."

I shook my head. "No. I'm pretty sure they don't even know Jo was dealing drugs. Let me call Jake. He's going to *love* hearing from me."

Rosie grinned. "I can't wait to hear this conversation."

Chapter 17

J ake picked up on the third ring. "Why does my chest hurt every time your number pops up on my phone?"

"Zoe's the doctor; you should probably ask her. Anyway, if you'd like a killer handed to you on a silver platter—well, a gray hospital bed—you'd better get over to this apartment."

There was silence on the other end of the line. "Are you joking?"

"As Judi Dench said to Pierce Brosnan in one of those Bond movies, I never joke about my work, James."

"Where are you? Why is the guy in a hospital bed? Is he secure?"

"Drug overdose, and probably. Dot's watching him."

"You left a seventy-something-year-old woman with a murderer?"

"To be fair, we didn't know he was a murderer

153

when she drove him to the hospital. And frankly, if it came down to it, I'd put my money on Dot any day of the week."

"How did you know he ODed?"

"We came to have a little chat, saw him lying on the living room floor, and decided to have a wee bit of a look around while we waited for him to come out of it. Or not. He was in pretty bad shape when we found him, though I figure Dot probably would have texted if he'd died."

I could practically *feel* Jake running his hands through his hair in frustration on the other end of the line. "Text me the address. I'll be there soon," was all he ended up saying before he ended the call.

"Gee, you'd think he'd be a little more grateful," I said to Rosie with a wry smile as I tapped away at my phone, letting Jake know where we were.

Rosie put the gun down on the table carefully and looked at it. "It's certainly not brand new, but it has been discharged."

"It's got to be the murder weapon. What are the odds that someone else linked to this case also owned the same caliber gun?"

"Well, this is America, so it's not *completely* outside the realm of possibility. But I agree. We're going to have to wait for ballistics to confirm. I'm not sure there's anything else in here worth looking at right now, anyway. I haven't seen a phone, which means he probably had it on him when he passed out. Dot will find it and find a way to get into it. Maybe there's something in his social media that will seal the deal.

Although if that gun is the one that killed Jo, he's cooked no matter what."

At that moment, a firm rap on the door told me Jake had shown up. "Charlie?"

I walked over and opened the door to find Jake glowering down at me, his eyes smoldering in anger. God, even when he was angry, he was still hot as hell. It wasn't fair.

"What have you got?" he asked.

Behind him was his partner, Liam. The fat older man had his thumbs tucked into his belt loops, and I didn't so much as glance at him. He was the one who had tried to Taser Dorothy but successfully Tasered me.

"Well hello to you too," I said airily to Jake, stepping aside to let him into the apartment. "I've got a lot more than you do. A murder weapon, for one. Well, we think, anyway. You're going to have to take it to your lab to find out for sure."

"Who lives here?" Jake asked, looking around. He acknowledged Rosie with a cold nod, and she crossed her arms in his direction in reply.

A self-satisfied smile crept up the corner of my mouth. "Name's Sean Sherman. Do you know who he is?"

"He was fired from the company where Jo Lismore worked," Jake replied, his mouth a grim line. "You say he's in the hospital?"

I pushed down the small wave of disappointment that washed over me. I had really hoped Jake wouldn't have had a clue who Sean was. But Jake wasn't *completely* incompetent. I did know that.

"He is," I replied. "Dot drove him. We figured it would be faster than waiting for an ambulance."

"He had a pulse when we came in, but it was very weak," Rosie added. "We couldn't wait."

Jake nodded, but Liam shook his head. "You should have called 911. That's what they're there for."

"It's good to know if I'm ever dying in front of you, you'll make sure to follow protocol exactly," Rosie replied flatly. "Luckily, of the two of us, I'd be willing to bet you're the one more likely to suffer from a heart attack."

"Was that a threat?" Liam snarled, taking a step toward Rosie, but Jake pressed a hand against his chest, holding him back.

"No, it was commentary on how you're a threat to any unattended donut boxes and not much else," Rosie shot back, and I didn't bother hiding my snicker.

"Look, Liam, why don't you go have a look outside and see if there's anything out there that can help us out?" Jake suggested.

"You're trying to get *me* out of here? They're the ones who broke into this place. We should be arresting them."

"I'm sure my best friend's mother, Julia Morgan, would love to hear all about it if you tried *that*," I said.

Liam's face paled. "She's... she's..."

I nodded smugly. It was nice to see Zoe's mom's name still made the blood of incompetent cops run cold. "That's right. So why don't you do as your partner suggests and get out of here? Besides, maybe if you knew how to actually run a murder investigation, you'd have gotten here first. It's not like I have access to all this information and you don't."

"You think you're smarter than me?" Liam snapped.

"I think there are ice cream cones that were dropped on the beach that are smarter than you."

He bared his teeth at me and opened his mouth to reply.

Jake interrupted first. "Enough," he barked. "Liam, outside. Charlie, stop making it worse." He practically shoved Liam out the door and closed it behind him then turned to us. "I swear, it's like trying to wrangle kindergarteners."

"He started it," I replied with a shrug.

Jake just stared at me in reply for at least five seconds before turning his mind back to the topic at hand. "You said you found the murder weapon?"

"On the counter," Rosie said, motioning with her head. "I found it behind the couch."

"I'm guessing those are the drugs he was partaking in?"

"Did you know he was an addict?" I asked, and Jake shook his head. "Did you know Jo was his dealer?"

This earned me a hard look from Jake. "Seriously?"

I nodded. "You didn't find any proof in her apartment?"

Jake swore. "No. You weren't lying this morning about her dealing drugs?"

"Well, really, this is all your fault. If whoever searched the bathroom hadn't been too scared to touch the tampon box—or hadn't simply assumed that the box of Advil actually had Advil in it—you would have found it."

Jake pressed his palm against his forehead and closed his eyes for a second. "Where are the drugs now?"

"At my place. I was going to hand them over to you after Zoe takes some in to work for testing. It looks like Percocet. Same as some of this stuff."

"You can't... you can't just keep a whole stash of drugs at your place, even if you're not going to deal them."

"Well duh. I was going to give them to you."

"And why haven't you yet?"

I shrugged. "Haven't gotten around to it. Didn't feel like you'd earned it."

"Earned it?" Jake fumed. "Do I really need to remind you this is a murder investigation?"

"You don't have to remind me. I'm the one finding all the evidence before you. I'll bring the drugs down to your place tonight, okay?"

"Fine. That's why you were being chased yesterday, isn't it? Someone was after the drugs left at Jo's place?"

I nodded. "Off the record, he ransacked it after you and your crew left, but before we got there. He spotted us entering and saw us leaving with more stuff than we had coming in. He tried to drive us off the road to get his goods back."

Jake raised an eyebrow. "And somehow, all of you ended up getting out of it okay?"

"That's right," I said quickly. I wasn't about to admit I'd been Tasered yet again. "We're a lot harder to handle than we look."

"Don't I know it," Jake muttered. "Okay, I think I'm caught up here. Jo was dealing, this guy was her supplier, and Sean was one of her customers. He got fired, felt bitter about it, bought a gun, and shot Jo. That's what you're thinking?"

"Correct," Rosie confirmed, stepping forward. "It's a nice gun too. Shame it's going to rot away in an evidence locker for the foreseeable future. We're assuming it's the murder weapon. It's the right caliber."

"It is," Jake confirmed, pulling an evidence bag from his back pocket. He grabbed a pen from the table and used it to pluck the gun off the table and drop it into the bag without touching it. "I'm going to have to take your prints for elimination purposes."

Rosie wiggled her fingers, displaying the gloves. "Way ahead of you."

"Good. Did you touch anything else in here?"

"No," I lied. I wasn't about to tell Jake I had samples of the drugs Sean had taken in my back pocket.

"Okay. I need you to get out of here. I'm going to call in a full crime-scene team. If Sean really is the killer and there's more evidence in here, I need to find it."

"You have to tell us if you find anything," I said.

Jake raised his eyebrows. "That's not how this works."

"Hey, I'm the one who called to basically gift you a murder weapon. The very least you can do is keep me in the loop."

"Again, that's not how police work works. I appreciate you calling this in and being a good citizen, but your involvement ends here. It's not just about finding the killer. It's also about making sure he's convicted and spends the rest of his life in prison. There's no point in me having this gun if I can't use it in court or if some shady defense lawyer manages to convince twelve people that I let a random couple not associated with law enforcement on my crime scene."

I opened my mouth to argue, but Rosie got there first. "He's right, Charlie. Come on, let's go find Dot and see if Sean is even still alive."

I nodded, and the two of us left the apartment.

"And stay away from Sean," Jake called out after us.

Liam stood at the corner of the sidewalk, his arms crossed, doing his best to look intimidating as a couple of teenagers walked past, snickering. Apparently, he wasn't doing a great job of it.

He scowled at Rosie and me as we walked past, and I took the opportunity to flip him the bird as we walked down the street. He called out something after me that I couldn't make out as a truck drove past, but I smiled to myself.

"I guess that's it, then," I said to Rosie. "I'm going to have to call Randall and let him know I solved the case."

Rosie nodded. "Congratulations. You did some excellent sleuthing, especially for an amateur."

"And I was only almost killed once."

"There is that. I have to say I'm disappointed that it's all over. I've been enjoying using my old skills again. You know, I haven't had to identify a gun on sight in nearly fifty years. I always kept up with the new models, of course. But it hasn't been necessary. I really did miss it. And of course, these days, with the way technology has evolved, there's a whole new layer to espionage and investigation. I don't know much about it, but luckily, Dot loves that sort of thing."

"Why don't you put up your own shingle?" I suggested with a shrug. "Surely you know enough old people who have bad things happen to them that you could manage it."

Rosie smiled. "Do you really think there's a club for the elderly out there where we all meet once a week, drink our Metamucil, and gossip about today's youth?"

"For all I know, there might be."

Rosie chuckled. "There's no such thing. Besides, much as with any generation, we all have our morons Sure, the *real* dumb ones are mostly dead by now. Duncan McCormack was one of them. It was a shame too. He was quite the looker. No brains, though. Thought he'd be clever by raising a tiger in his backyard. He thought the movie studios would want to use it when they shoot out here. Unfortunately for Duncan, the tiger decided he was more than just a snack, he was a whole meal."

"I think I remember my parents talking about that," I said slowly.

"Probably because after eating Duncan, the tiger figured he'd have a gander at what a life of freedom was like. For four days, the tiger roamed free in Maui while the authorities tried to figure out how to catch him."

"Did they manage it?"

"Oh, yeah. There was tons of panic first, though. He went for a swim in the ocean near Honomanu one day. People thought it was going to drive tourists away, that no one wanted to experience a real-life *Jaws* situation. The mayor wanted to carpet bomb the forest, but luckily for everybody, that was quickly nixed as an idea. Eventually, he ended up on a property in Wailua. Faced down the woman living there. She smacked him on the nose with a newspaper, wrapped her dog's leash around his neck, and kept him in the yard until the authorities got there. They packed him up in a crate, and he spent the rest of his days in a sanctuary on the mainland somewhere."

"Wow."

"Anyway, what was I talking about? That's right, morons. Just because I'm the same age as other people doesn't mean I find them interesting. Besides, if I were to get a private investigator's license, I'd have to have my fingerprints put on file. And you can understand why I'd like to avoid that."

"That's a good point. It's too bad."

"Well, if you should decide to go down that line of work, I'd be happy to freelance for you," Rosie said with a wink. "And so would Dot. According to her, you can only hack into the CIA's servers so many times before it gets boring."

I snorted. "I bet."

"I think she's trying to alter some files to convince them to overthrow the wrong South American country next, but you'd have to ask her the details."

"I'm pretty sure I don't *want* to know the details."

"That's probably best for everybody."

Chapter 18

Despite the walk to the hospital having been less than a mile long, by the time we reached the front doors, I was drenched in sweat, and my hair felt like it was plastered to my head. That was Maui humidity for you, even with winter just around the corner.

We walked through the front doors at Emergency, and I breathed a sigh of relief as the air conditioning blasted me with cool air. How anybody lived in this place before aircon was invented was beyond me.

Dot was seated at one of the plain metal chairs in the waiting area, tapping away on her phone. She looked up and nodded when she spotted us.

"So, did he die?" I asked, plonking myself down on the chair across from Dot.

"From what I've heard from the doctor, he's going to make it."

"Good. It's just in time for him to get arrested," Rosie said.

"So it's solved?"

"In all likelihood. Rosie found a gun behind the couch that was the same caliber as the one that killed Jo."

"You have to love people so out of their minds on drugs that they don't even bother getting rid of the murder weapon," Dot said with a shake of her head. "Well, at least now you'll get to collect your money."

"And I'll be making sure you both get your cut this time," I said, holding up a hand before they could protest. "I mean it. I never would have figured this out without you."

"Well, that's very kind of you," Dot said. "Frankly, I'm a bit disappointed this case has come to an end."

"I told Rosie she should put up her shingle. Maybe you should do the same," I offered with a grin.

Dot shook her head. "Oh, no. I don't want to draw that much attention to myself."

"Yes, you're obviously such an introvert."

"As much as I may seem comfortable around you, I very much am. I much prefer the company of computers to people, even when they're paying me. Rosie is the social butterfly of the two of us."

"Well, if another case like this falls into my lap, I'll call you. Now, what do you say we go home and take a well-deserved break?"

"Sounds like a great plan," Rosie said.

"I guess I took this off Sean for nothing, then," Dot said with a frown, pulling out an iPhone with a completely smashed screen.

"Well, if you want to look at it, you should," I said.

"You never know. But if you find anything that proves Sean's our killer, I guess email it to Jake or something."

Dot snickered. "If I think he deserves it."

"That's the spirit."

I HAD DOT AND ROSIE DROP ME OFF AT OLIVIA'S garage before heading home so that I could pick up Queenie. Her address was on West Waiko Road in Waikapu, only about three miles up the hill from the hospital. The bungalow she worked out of was old, with peeling paint on the shabby exterior, and the yard was home to about four different cars in various states of disrepair. Queenie was in the open garage. I hopped out, said goodbye to Dot and Rosie, and walked toward the car.

"Hey," Olivia said as soon as she spotted me. She'd been on the driver's side of the car "You sure put this girl to the test, didn't you?"

"Sorry," I said with an apologetic shrug. "I didn't really mean to do that on day one."

"Cars were meant to be driven," Olivia replied. "We can always put them back together after. And if we can't, well, there are lots of other cars out there, and we can always use the parts that do still work. Frankly, I'd be disappointed if you bought as incredible a car as this one and just drove her along South Kihei Road while doing the speed limit. How did this happen, anyway?"

"A drug dealer who thought I had his stash tried to

run me off the road. His Toyota ended up in the ocean."

Olivia grinned. "Now that's what I like to hear. I'm just about done here. Give me about twenty more minutes, and she'll be good to go. You're lucky I had all the parts you needed in stock. I have a soft spot for Jeeps, so I tend to get whatever I can for them."

Just then, a Rottweiler ran out from the house, his stumpy tail wagging, a huge smile on his face. He made a beeline for me, tongue hanging outside his mouth next to the tennis ball he carried.

"That's Egg McMuffin, but his friends call him Egg," Olivia said.

"He looks terrifying," I said as Egg dropped his tennis ball at my feet, looking up at me expectantly. I reached down and picked up the slobber-covered ball and threw it as hard as I could up to the other end of the yard, past the cars on the grass. Egg sprinted toward the fence, gleefully chasing it.

"Oh, he is," Olivia said with a laugh as she tinkered with the side mirror. "He's a rescue. I got him when he was about six months old, and he hasn't left my side since. He was found on the street eating someone's leftover McDonalds. That's how he got his name."

Egg ran back over, almost galloping with uneven legs as he happily dropped the ball and wagged his tail again in anticipation. We settled into a routine, with me throwing the ball for him while I chatted with Olivia.

"So how long have you lived on Maui?" I asked.

"My whole life. I was born in the bathroom," Olivia said, motioning with her head toward the main house. "My parents were hippies who didn't believe in hospitals. Unfortunately, breast cancer certainly believed in my mom. And then dad had a heart attack when I was twenty."

"I'm sorry," I said. "My dad died of cancer when I was sixteen. I know what you went through."

Olivia nodded. "You really do get it. Dad's the one who showed me how to fix cars. I was their only child, and he figured there was no reason he couldn't teach his little girl how to work her way around a garage. He thought paying to get a car service was a total rip-off, and he wasn't about to let his daughter live her life without knowing the same things he did. Turns out I liked it so much I decided to become one of those rip-off mechanics he was trying to avoid."

I laughed. "Dad loved surfing. He always wanted to get me in the water, but I didn't want to. Despite growing up here, I always liked the beach more than the ocean. I regret not learning from him now."

Olivia gave me a sad smile. "Yeah. Dad tried turning me into a football player too. He was a running back for the Buckeyes. The only time he ever lived on the mainland. He hated it. Said he never wanted to see snow again. But I never took to football. I wish I had."

"At least the two of you had cars."

"That we did," she said with a smile. "And it pays the bills these days. I have a pretty solid clientele of primarily women who don't trust male mechanics not to rip them off. They know I'll give them a fair deal and that I know what I'm doing."

"You obviously do," I said approvingly.

"Anyway, you're ready to go."

"Thanks," I said with a grin. "Can you email me the invoice? I'm getting costs covered on this."

"Sure thing. Come on, Egg. Time to go back into the house. It's getting dark, and it's time for your dinner anyway."

Egg's ears perked up at the sound of the word "dinner," and I laughed as I watched him drop his ball, the toy immediately forgotten, and sprint right back into the house.

"Keys are in the ignition," Olivia said. "Let's see if you can make it two days without bringing it back to me this time."

I laughed. "A girl can dream. Thanks again."

Olivia gave me a casual salute and headed into the house while I climbed behind the wheel of my car. The crack in the windshield was gone, and I actually had a side mirror again on the passenger side, which was a big improvement on just a few hours ago.

I turned the engine over, and it roared to a start, and I grinned as I pulled back out onto the road, my ride back to being in tip-top condition.

And the best part was I wasn't even paying the bill.

I PULLED INTO THE PARKING LOT AT THE APARTMENT building—my heart did a little skip for joy as I realized it was *my* apartment building and not my mother's home—and headed upstairs. As soon as I stepped through the door, my mouth dropped open.

"Holy crap!"

Zoe gave me a sheepish grin from the kitchen, where she was busy stacking plates in the cabinets. "Does it look okay?"

"If the whole doctor thing doesn't work out as a career for you, I vote you become one of those people who renovates houses for people on HGTV," I replied. "This looks incredible. How did you do all this so quickly?"

What had started out as a semi furnished apartment with the bare minimum in place was now a warm, welcoming home. Ivory-and-gold blackout curtains stopped the afternoon sun from turning this place into an oven. A warm cream-colored area rug was now tucked beneath the front legs of the couch, and a live-edge acacia coffee table sat in front of it, topped with one of Zoe's hardcover books featuring cool close-up pictures of birds. I had seen that book before; only some of the birds were super creepy and weird. Most were adorable. It was a good book.

"I take it you like it?"

"It looks awesome."

"Great. I'm going to get a bit of art to put on the walls, and it should be perfect. How did your investigation go?"

"Well, we found the killer. At least, I'm about ninety-five percent sure we did."

"No kidding. Good job. Who was it?"

"One of the guys Jo was supplying with pills, who she fired."

"Well, no lack of motive."

"Exactly. Rosie found the gun he used behind the couch. Jake's testing it now. Oh, speaking of, it turns out he's one of our neighbors too."

"Jake, really? The cop who tried to help me when that creep came after me?"

"That's the one."

"Well, on the bright side, he seemed okay, all things considered."

"He does seem to actually care about crime in this town, and making changes in the way it's tackled," I admitted. "Still, he also seems to care about keeping me out of the investigations."

A smile appeared in the corner of Zoe's mouth. "I mean, you can't really blame him for that. As long as his partner doesn't show up too often, it should be okay."

"Yeah, I guess so. I also met a lady down the hall named Jesper who used to be a bigshot surfer until a shark bit off her leg. Leslie knows her well. Apparently, she has a habit of exaggerating stories a little—just a heads-up."

"Thanks," Zoe chuckled. "She sounds fun."

"She certainly is. Now, you've spent the whole day working, right? And I found a murderer. What do you say we grab some pizza and watch a bit of TV?"

"That sounds fantastic. Especially since I haven't had a chance to get any groceries yet. *Jeopardy!* starts in about twenty minutes. The pizza should arrive just in time to watch it."

"Uh, yeah, that's exactly what I was going to suggest," I lied.

Zoe rolled her eyes good-naturedly at me. "You can choose where we get the pizza from if we get to watch *Jeopardy!* when it gets here."

"Deal. Although you probably know what the better pizza places on the island are. You tell me the place, I get to choose the toppings."

Zoe laughed. "See? This is why we work so well together."

I had to say, she was right.

Chapter 19

I had gotten completely creamed by Zoe while watching *Jeopardy!*—I had never even *heard* of Bloemfontein, the South African city that was the answer to Final Jeopardy, but Zoe got it instantly. I decided that instead of getting another slice of pizza, I was going to call Randall. After all, I had to keep him up to date on the case, and the fact that we basically had found the killer was a big development.

"Hello?" he answered on the second ring.

"Hi, Randall. It's Charlie."

"How is the case going? Have you found out who killed Jo yet?"

"I'm almost certain I have," I replied. "It was Sean Sherman. I went to his apartment this afternoon, where I found him having overdosed on drugs. He's recovering at the hospital now, but I found a .38 caliber gun in his home, the same caliber that killed Jo. I alerted Jacob Llewellyn, the detective in charge of your daughter's case, and he's taken the gun in for ballistics testing. I assume he's also arrested Sean Sherman for your daughter's murder."

There was silence on the other end of the line for a moment. "Thank you."

"It's not a sure thing just yet. Jake and I agree that it's very likely the gun will come back as the murder weapon, but the test hasn't been done yet. When I find out the results, I'll give you a call."

"Of course. I understand. Thank you for keeping me in the loop, Charlie. I really appreciate it."

I hung up the phone and sighed. "You know, I don't think doctors get enough credit for having to tell someone their family member died. I just got to give that man the news that the guy who almost certainly killed his daughter has been arrested, and I *still* feel like crap, because I know that even though it's good news, it's never going to bring back Jo."

Zoe gave me a small smile of sympathy. "No, it's not easy. But thanks to you, that family's going to get closure. They're never going to have to walk past an unfamiliar face in the grocery store and ask themselves if that's the person who took their daughter's life. Or worse, ask themselves when they're having dinner with friends or employees."

I nodded. "That's a good point. Still, it feels a bit like a hollow victory. You know what would be better than being a detective? Being a superhero. At least then you'd get to stop crimes before they happen."

"You know I'll support you in any career path you choose, but I have to ask: what exactly do you think your superpower would be?"

"I don't know. I guess I'm just so cool I'd instantly shock anybody bad into submission?"

"That's the worst superpower I've ever heard."

"Well, this is real life. Batman didn't have any superpowers. I'll do what he does."

"Right. If only we'd gotten a three-bedroom place, you could have turned one of them into a Batcave."

"Now you're getting it. But I'd need a different name. Sure, there are bats in Hawaii, but I'd want to be something cuter. And everyone thinks of Christian Bale when they think of Batman."

"You could be Taser-woman," Zoe said with a grin.

I stuck my tongue out at her. "What about Turtle Woman? Everyone thinks of turtles when they think of Hawaii."

Zoe lifted a single brow. "I'm not sure people associate turtles with heroic deeds."

"You're obviously forgetting about the Ninja Turtles."

"Sure, but you're not nearly good enough an artist to join their ranks."

I blew out a breath of air. "You're not helping. Also, you're a nerd."

Zoe shrugged. "Super Monk Seal?"

"Okay, no, I liked it more when you weren't giving suggestions. Ugh. There's just no cool superhero names that remind me of Hawaii. I don't want people associating me with a seal. Or a macadamia nut. Or a pineapple. There's just no way to make a pineapple sexy, and if I'm going to be a superhero, I want to be a sexy one."

"I feel like you're putting too much thought into this for a hypothetical, and then I start to wonder if you're thinking that being a superhero might actually be a viable career path for you."

"Well, no, but I kind of wish it was."

Zoe opened her mouth to reply, but before she did, my ringtone interrupted. I glanced at the screen; it was Dot.

"One sec." I slid my thumb across the screen and moved the phone to my ear. "Dot. What's up?"

"We have a problem. You need to come over, now."

"Be there in ten."

I hung up the phone and turned to Zoe. "Bad news. I've got to go."

"What's wrong?"

"I'm not sure, but Dot says we have a situation."

"Well, there's no one better for the job than you, the Powerful Pineapple," Zoe said with a mischievous grin.

"I told you, pineapples aren't sexy," I called out as I headed to the front door to put my shoes back on. "I'm going to be a sexy superhero, damn it."

I could hear Zoe still cackling with laughter as I left the apartment and headed down the stairs to the parking garage. I made a mental note to drop the other drugs off at Jake's place when I got home.

I PULLED INTO A VISITOR'S SPOT IN DOT'S BUILDING a few minutes later and headed up the stairs. Rosie pulled the door open about half a second after I knocked.

"What's up?" I asked, walking into the apartment.

Dot was at her computer, dwarfed by the screens in front of her. "Come have a look at this," she said without turning around, and I headed over to the computer.

A video popped open on one of the screens. It was blurry and shaky, and it looked like it had been taken inside a club. Lights flashed and music pounded, and I couldn't make out much of anything. Then the screen more or less focused on a face I recognized: Sean Sherman.

He was either drunk or stoned out of his mind. Or both. He slurred his words as he grinned at the camera, which kept changing angles.

"Jo, this video is for you. You're a real bitch, you know that? But the thing is, I don't need your drugs or your stupid-ass job. You got where you did because of your dad, not because you're better than me. You dumb slut. Look at what you're missing."

The camera moved downward, and Dot turned it off, but not before I got an eyeful at a part of Sean I'd have been much happier going my whole life without seeing.

"Oh, gross. What a terrible day to have functioning eyes. Why do men have to turn everything into a dick pic? Or in this case, a dick video?"

"It's the zoom lens," Dot said. "Anyway, this video is why I called you here."

"Really? Because there's *much* better porn on the internet if that's what you're after."

Dot shot me a look. "Honey, I can find porn online for kinks you don't even know exist."

"Okay, I think we're getting a little off topic," Rosie interrupted. "I don't consider myself a prude, but under no circumstances do I want you to go through that list, Dot."

"Right. No, I called you here because of the time stamp. Sean Sherman took this video at the same time Jo Lismore was killed."

"You're joking." My heart sank as I realized the implications immediately.

"I wish I was," Dot said, her mouth a grim line. "There are four videos on this phone taken between ten and eleven the night Jo was killed. They're all along the same vein. He sent them to Jo on Snapchat."

I ran a hand through my hair. "You're right. That means he can't be our killer. Do you know where he was when he took the footage?"

"As much as I might pretend I'm all up with what the kids are doing these days, that one's a bit beyond even me," Dot said. "I haven't got a clue what club that is, and I was hoping you'd be able to help with that."

"Send me a copy of the video, but please, for everyone's sake, trim out the... less savory bits. I'll see if I can find someone who can identify this club for us.

I haven't been back on the island for long enough to know."

"Will do," Dot said. "In fact, as much as I hate to say it, you should probably turn the whole phone over to the police. They're going to need to see this too."

"Right. Otherwise, Sean Sherman is spending the rest of his life in jail."

I took the phone from Dot and slipped it into my pocket. Jake wasn't going to be pleased. But hey, he'd had access to the same information I did. It wasn't my fault his crew hadn't found Sean Sherman first.

"Yes, Sean might have his problems, but it doesn't appear he's the killer," Rosie said. "Still, we will want to confirm."

"Agreed. I don't think he has the mental capacity to change the time stamp on his revenge videos, but given that he worked in computer science, I wouldn't put it entirely past him," Dot said. "That's why I want to find out where the club is. We need to confirm it was him."

"Okay, leave it with me. And what if everything is as it appears? How did Sean Sherman end up with the gun that I think it's still safe to say killed Jo Lismore?"

"That's the million-dollar question, isn't it?" Rosie said. "Someone obviously wanted us to think Sean Sherman was the killer. But who?"

"Let's figure that out after we confirm that he was for sure sending dick videos at the club while Jo was being shot," I said. "We've gotten ahead of ourselves once already. I don't want to do it again."

A few minutes I headed back down to the car,

swearing inwardly. I had been so convinced that Sean Sherman was the killer. It made perfect sense. That gun *had* to be the murder weapon. Surely there weren't two people linked with Jo Lismore who had the same caliber gun that was used to kill her hanging around. Or maybe I just underestimated how many guns were on the island.

I headed back home, feeling dejected and disappointed. Halfway there, my phone binged to indicate I had a text. I opened it as I headed up the stairs; Dot had sent through the video. Luckily, she had edited out the worst parts.

"What happened?" Zoe asked when I got back in, still munching on some pizza on the couch.

"There's video proof that Sean Sherman might not be the killer. Apparently he was at a club when Jo was shot. Do you recognize this place?"

I handed the phone to Zoe, who looked at the video a few times. "Ew, is he about to pull out his   "

"Yup," I replied dryly. "And in the unedited version he does exactly that. So, you're welcome."

"Ugh. Why even are men? Anyway, yeah, I know where this is. I think, anyway. Yeah, I'm pretty sure. I haven't been there in a few years, but it's the Horny Turtle. That should be your superhero name."

I raised my eyebrows while laughing. "Are you kidding me? Maui has a club called the Horny Turtle? Who's their target market, fourteen-year-old boys?"

"Yeah, the crowd trends younger. It's mostly undergrads with fake IDs and forty-year-olds trying to get with the nineteen-year-olds."

"Wow, this place sounds like a winner."

"I'm honestly surprised they haven't been permanently shut down yet. It's the sort of place where someone can get away with doing drugs without being noticed, too. Might be why it was Sean Sherman's haunt."

I smiled at Zoe. "Are you up for a fun night of pretending we're nineteen?"

She raised her eyebrows at me. "Look, we both aged very well, but we didn't age *that* well."

"Okay, fine. Pretending we're twenty-two."

"Well, the lighting isn't great outside the club, so I think we might be able to pull that off. What are we going to do? If it involves anything illegal, you're on your own."

"Don't worry," I replied with a shake of my head. "We're just going to go in there and ask the staff if they recognize him and if they saw him that night."

"Cool. Well, at least I've never been kicked out of a club for being a total buzzkill before, so might as well cross that off my bucket list tonight."

"Oh, please. I'd be willing to bet you've never been kicked out of a club for anything before."

"Fine," Zoe admitted. "Let me go see if there's anything in my closet that might be remotely appropriate for clubbing in my late twenties."

"Don't forget to slather on the makeup," I called out as I went to my own room to do the same.

Chapter 20

There was a part of me that liked to think I wasn't too old for clubbing. After all, I was still young and hip and cool. I followed meme pages on Facebook, and sometimes there were even Gen Zers posting. Okay, not often. I didn't think a lot of them were on Facebook anymore. But still, if they were, I was sure they'd understand how hilarious the meme about *Friends* that I'd seen the other day was.

Gen Z knew what *Friends* was, right?

Okay, if that hadn't convinced me that maybe, just *maybe* my days of being a cool young adult were quickly coming to an end, the sight that stared back at me from the mirror certainly did. I was wearing a tube dress that had probably stopped fitting me properly a year ago and had almost certainly gone out of style at least six or seven years before that. My hoop earrings were supposed to make me look fancy, but instead, they just made me look like I'd hopped right out of a magazine published in 2002. I'd overdone my makeup, thinking it would make me look sexy, but I looked more like the clown from *It* than an "it" girl.

Well, if worse came to worst, I could always bribe the bouncer to let us in. Hopefully, the light was really, *really* bad.

I trudged back out into the living room to find Zoe waiting for me. She looked super cute in a shimmery silver dress and heels, and she'd done her makeup to look a little bit like a kitten, which gave her that younger look we were going for.

"How is your nerdy butt so much better at this than me? I'm supposed to be the cool one in this relationship."

Zoe laughed. "You have no idea how hard med students can party."

"Obviously not. Okay, let's get this over with."

I texted Dot and Rosie to let them know where we were going then headed down to the car with Zoe.

"I ran the test for you today," Zoe said. "It was a mixture of oxycodone and acetaminophen but laced with fentanyl. Not real Percocet."

"Is that common on the island, the fentanyl? I know it's getting to be a bit of a problem in Seattle."

Zoe nodded. "Yeah, it's become an issue the last few years. I know there's been a campaign at the hospital aimed at encouraging users to carry naloxone with them, which can reverse the effects of fentanyl."

"I wonder if Jo knew she was dealing bad stuff," I mused.

Zoe shrugged. "Her supplier might know, if he'd give you an honest answer."

"Yeah, I'm sure Dot and Rosie know how to keep tabs on him, at the very least. We'll be able to track him down. Mind if I stop at Jake's apartment and give him the rest of the drugs, then?"

"Sure, but I'm going to wait in the car."

"Here you go," I said, tossing her the keys to Queenie.

Zoe smiled and gave me a quick wave as she headed down the hall while I went back to the apartment and grabbed the rest of the drugs.

I walked down and knocked on Jake's door. He answered a moment later, and his eyebrows rose as he looked me up and down.

"Special delivery," I said, handing over the box of tampons and the Advil. "Please don't comment on the outfit."

"Wasn't going to. And thanks, but it's not my time of the month for another week," he replied, taking them from me. "This is all of it?"

"All of it we didn't have tested. If you want me to save you some time, they're not real Percocet. It's fake and laced with fentanyl."

Jake frowned. "That's a lot of pills. It sure explains a lot."

"Let me guess: Sean's overdose was on fentanyl?"

Jake nodded. "Yeah. They got him the naloxone in time, at least, and he's going to make a full recovery from his jail cell."

"Has your ballistics report come back?"

"Not the whole thing; that won't be until tomorrow. But I spoke to the technician, and he told me that it was the gun that killed Jo."

I nodded. "Okay. Thanks."

I turned to leave, but Jake called out to me. "Out of curiosity, where are you going?"

"Just tying up some loose ends. Nothing you need to worry about."

"That's funny, because you look like you're ready to go clubbing, and I didn't exactly peg you as that type."

"Well, I guess you're just not as good a detective as you thought you were," I said with a wink.

And with that, I strutted down the hall and to the car, where Zoe was waiting.

THE HORNY TURTLE WAS LOCATED IN LAHAINA. Formerly Hawaii's capital and the center of the whaling trade in the nineteenth century, the town had kept a lot of its old-timey charm. But it was also a prime tourist location and was one of the most crowded places on the island. It was also home to some of the most popular nightclubs for that same reason. But right now, well after ten o'clock and in the middle of shoulder season, the main road was practically empty.

I parked a few blocks away from Front Street, and Zoe and I walked the rest of the way.

"What are we going to do if they don't let us in?" Zoe asked on the way, biting her bottom lip.

"If we've got enough confidence, that won't be a problem. And if there's one thing I have, it's confidence."

"Here's hoping," Zoe muttered.

We reached Front Street, with its old colonial-style buildings, and it wasn't hard to find the Horny Turtle. The bass coming from the music inside was so loud it probably triggered the Richter scale most nights, and colorful lights shone from the second-story balcony onto the closed facades of the nearby stores. It looked as if the Horny Turtle occupied the second story of one of the buildings, with the tenants occupying the space below running a vegan bakery and café.

A small door next to the café served as the entrance, and a guy who reminded me way too much of Dwayne Johnson guarded it. The lights reflected off his bald head, and he stood with his legs apart, arms folded across his puffed-out chest, doing his best to look more important than he really was.

I strutted toward him with Zoe right behind me.

As we reached the man, he looked us up and down. "Sorry, we're full."

I scoffed. "Please. It's a Thursday in November. We both know you're not full. Besides, what's wrong with us? We look ready to party."

"Aren't your days of hard partying behind you?"

"Excuse me?" Oh, man. I knew I wasn't going to pass for twenty-two anymore, but this was ridiculous.

"This is an establishment with a certain reputation," the man said. "I'm afraid it would set a bad precedent letting two women like you in."

"Oh, I know exactly what kind of reputation this place has," I said, stepping forward and jabbing a finger into the man's chest. "Problem is we're not seventeen with fake IDs anymore, trying to have some fun before one of the forty-year-old creeps you let into this place does his best to roofie our drinks."

"Hey," the man said, obviously offended. But before he had a chance to say anything else, Rosie and Dot shuffled over.

"Excuse me, excuse me, emergency," Rosie said, shuffling Dot toward the door.

"Sorry, this is private property," the bouncer said, moving between the two older women and the door, blocking their access.

"Listen, son, I have irritable bowel syndrome, and it's coming on real bad," Dot said.

"She had too much prune juice with dinner," Rosie said, shaking her head. "You really must let us in."

"Ohh, I feel like there's a mouse head poking out of me," Dot cried out, and I mashed my fist into my mouth to keep from laughing while the bouncer's expression turned to one of horror.

"Fine. Go, go! Bathrooms are on the right when you get up there. Go!"

"That's not even how IBS presents," Zoe muttered in a low voice behind me.

"Thank you, young man," Rosie said, handing him a caramel from her pocket before leading Dot through the club door and up the stairs. Apparently, she was taking her role of the kindly old grandmother *very* seriously.

"If I threaten to pee on you, will you let us in, too?" I asked when the door closed behind the two older women, and he shot me a sidelong glance.

"Sorry. I'm not letting you in. It wouldn't be a good look."

"Yes, how dare you let in a couple women who are almost *thirty*," Zoe said, rolling her eyes. "Come on, Charlie."

I let Zoe lead me away from the club, but I was still stewing. "If we were men, we could be fifteen years older, and he'd have let us in."

"Yeah, the misogyny there was pretty obvious," Zoe agreed. "Still, there was no point in arguing with him."

"Well, I'm not giving up."

"Really? Can't we just go home? After all, Dot and Rosie got in there just fine. They'll get any information you need."

I shook my head. "Now it's a matter of principle. I'm not ready to roll over and go into a nursing home just yet. Besides, I want to stand on that balcony and wave at the bouncer."

"Of course you do," Zoe said with a sigh. "Okay, do you have an actual plan?"

"Plans are overrated."

"I can tell this is going to go extremely well."

"Have a little faith."

"All right, well, whatever you come up with had better not include breaking any laws."

"Okay, come on," I said, motioning for Zoe to

follow me. I headed up the alley to the side of the building. Maybe there was a rear entrance we could use.

While there was, it was soundly locked.

"Do you have any chloroform in that bag by any chance?"

"No, I don't, because I'm not a serial killer. Besides, it doesn't actually work like the movies. You can't knock someone out in seconds using it; it would take at least five minutes."

I breathed air out of my cheeks. "Maybe we can scale the side of the building and get onto the second story that way."

"You know what? I think I'll just call the ambulance now so they're ready and waiting when you settle on an idea."

"I don't see you coming up with anything."

"That's because my suggestion is that we wait for Rosie and Dot to get the information we need. It's legal, painless, and doesn't involve sneaking into a building we're not allowed into."

"Really? You're going to let those two old ladies outsmart us? They got in; surely we can too."

Zoe shrugged. "I mean, I'll happily follow you, but I'm not nearly as competitive as you are. If they get the info and we don't, then so be it."

"Besides, that guy was a pig. He wouldn't let us in because we're in our late twenties. If we were men, it wouldn't have been a problem. We should have thought of that before and dressed up as dudes. Then we would have been let in."

"That's probably true," Zoe admitted.

I looked around to see what options there were. We needed a distraction, something to get the bouncer away from that door. Unfortunately, this was a standard alley behind a dumpy club. There was an abandoned shopping cart, a dumpster, and random trash and empty cardboard boxes here and there.

"What about a lighter? Do you have one of those?"

Zoe narrowed her eyes at me. "I'm not entirely sure I like the sound of that."

"Is that a yes?"

"No, but I think I might have a small box of matches in here," Zoe said, rifling through her purse. "I grabbed them from your mom's place so I could light my candles."

"Perfect."

"This doesn't sound an awful lot like a plan that's entirely law abiding."

"Don't worry, it's only going to be a bit of light arson."

"You are *not* setting this building on fire."

"No, of course I'm not."

"Okay, just checking."

"I'm going to fill this shopping cart with junk and set *it* on fire."

"Oh boy."

"You don't have to help. You can wait in the car if you want. But trust me, it'll be fine."

I started loading the cart with everything I could

find that looked flammable. Cardboard boxes, old clothes, that sort of thing.

"Come into the hospital while I'm working tomorrow, and I'll give you a tetanus booster."

"How do you know I'm not up to date on that one?" I asked.

Zoe shot me a look. "A wild stab in the dark. Which, incidentally, is the greatest cause of people needing tetanus shots."

"Fine," I muttered. She was right; I didn't think I'd ever had a tetanus shot.

After a few minutes, the cart was loaded with as much flammable material as I could find, made all the better by the discovery of a couple firecrackers and a half can of gasoline. I sprinkled the gasoline over the whole setup, and I was getting ready to push the cart out to the street when Zoe grabbed me.

"Hold on. The way you have the firecrackers set up, they're going to blow right away. You want to give them a few seconds. She adjusted the setup, looked at the work, then nodded. "There. That will give you a little bit of time before the firecrackers go off for added surprise."

"Thanks," I said with a grin. "Okay. I'm going to light this on fire and push it out into the street. It's a slight downhill, so it should keep going, no problem. When the bouncer goes to investigate, we sneak in through the door behind him."

"Got it," Zoe said.

The two of us carried the cart to the end of the alley to keep it quiet—the abandoned shopping cart wasn't exactly well oiled—and when it was in place, Zoe handed me the small box of matches. I pulled one, lit it, and dropped it in the middle of the cart.

Flames rushed upward with a whoosh, and I instinctively took a step backward as the heat warmed my face. "Here goes nothing," I said, grabbing the cart by the handle and stepping out onto the street, pushing it down toward the club.

The cart began picking up speed, and Zoe and I peered around the corner carefully, watching as it wobbled toward the bouncer, who gaped at the flaming cart. One of the firecrackers chose that instant to go off, causing the cart to veer back out toward the road, avoiding the bouncer. Still, he stared after it, looking up the street.

Deciding it needed to be stopped, the bouncer started chasing the cart as it picked up speed down Front Street. As soon as he left his post, Zoe and I ran to the club door. I yanked it open, and the two of us stumbled inside, quickly climbing the dingy stairs leading to the Horny Turtle.

Chapter 21

The music pounded so loudly I could barely hear myself think. It was some EDM remix of the latest Drake hit that made it sound like every other remix ever played in clubs. Why didn't someone ask the DJ to turn it down?

Okay, maybe I *was* getting a little bit too old for this.

The majority of the club's interior was a dance floor, where it looked like half the population of Hawaii was busy grinding away. Sure enough, the patrons fell into one of two categories: young enough that even I knew their IDs were fake or old enough to be their dads. Against the far wall at the back of the building was a DJ booth, from which lasers shot out in a rainbow of colors.

The lighting on the dance floor was a mixture of blue and red, pulsing every few seconds as revelers grinded against each other.

Hanging from the ceiling was a giant turtle, at least

ten feet long, looking kind of stoned like the one in *Finding Nemo*.

Rosie was at the bar against the wall on the far left, talking to the woman behind it. I tapped Zoe on the arm and motioned over there, and the two of us headed that way, pushing past all the dancers on the floor. The stools on either side of Rosie were empty; apparently, the few people around who wanted a break from the dancing didn't want to sit next to my geriatric friend. What were they afraid of, that her oldness would rub off on them?

Zoe and I each took one of the stools on either side of Rosie, who didn't so much as bat an eyelid at the sight of us, while the bartender squinted at Rosie's phone while nodding slowly. She had a half-sleeve tattoo and dyed black hair, along with a septum ring. She looked like the kind of woman who wouldn't take any of the crap doled out by the clientele here. "Yeah, he was here that night," she said loudly to be heard over the thumping beat. "We had to kick him out."

"Did you see what he was filming?"

The bartender nodded. "Yup. One of the other patrons spotted it and complained. He was sitting at one of the tables over in the corner."

"And you're one hundred percent sure it was that night?" Rosie asked.

"Sure am. That was the last night I worked. And I remember waking up the next day and seeing the news about the woman's body washing up on shore. Did he know her?"

"He did," I confirmed, adding myself to the conversation. "At what time did you kick him out?"

"Around eleven maybe?" the bartender replied.

"There's no way it was earlier?" Rosie asked. "It couldn't have been around ten?"

"No, it was definitely later than that. I remember we were starting to get busy, so ten was too early."

"Wait, this place isn't busy yet?" I asked.

The bartender grinned at me. "Honey, we like to test the fire department's occupancy limits almost every night. One day, I swear someone's going to go through the floor. The foundations of this building just aren't that good."

I looked over at the dance floor. It already looked pretty full; I couldn't imagine it getting even busier. Then I spotted Tommy, Jo's ex. He was grinding aggressively against a woman who looked like she was trying to get away from him as fast as she could. Tommy, for his part, didn't seem to notice that he was basically estrogen repellent.

It was too bad I had called his roommate and his alibi had checked out; he had been at home all night playing video games the night Jo was killed.

"Was that guy here with anyone that night?" Rosie asked, motioning back to the video of Sean.

The waitress shook her head. "Nope. Total loner. The jackoffs always are."

"Wait, this isn't the first time you've had to deal with something like this?" Zoe asked, aghast.

The bartender laughed. "I'm not sure it's even on my top ten list of gross things I've seen here. But the tips I make in a night make it worth it. Speaking of, hold on."

She went down to the other end of the bar to take an order, and the three of us put our heads together to be able to speak without having to scream at one another.

"Sounds like that's settled," I said. "It couldn't have been Sean."

"No, he was definitely here when Jo was shot," Rosie said. "We have to look elsewhere for our killer."

"But then the question becomes how did the gun get into his apartment?" Zoe asked. "After all, it's still the same gun, right?"

"You're asking the right question," Rosie said. "Let's see if the bartender knows anything else that can help us."

I looked around for Dot. After all, both Rosie and Dot had entered, but only Rosie was at the bar. My eyes scanned the dance floor, a part of me worried that I was about to see a seventy-something woman grinding against a guy who could be her grandson. But she wasn't there. Then I spotted a flash of silver hair up in the DJ booth. There was Dot, wearing a giant pair of over-the-ear headphones, tapping away at the computer.

Suddenly, the music changed. Instead of any old EDM track, the music changed to a Jock Jams Megamix that could not have possibly been more nineties. I cringed, expecting a revolt from the dance floor, but to my surprise, a chorus of cheers erupted instead.

Apparently, the crowd was into this.

The bartender came back at that moment, and I focused my attention back on her. "Is there anything else you can tell us about this guy?"

"Apart from what he was drinking, I don't think so. Sorry."

"Okay, thanks."

The bartender headed off to serve her next few customers, and the three of us went to grab Dot from the stage and head back home.

"I don't see why I had to come back with you," Dot grumbled as the three of us headed back down the stairs. "I was enjoying myself. Besides, the DJ owes me."

"He owes you?" I asked, raising my eyebrows.

"He couldn't figure out how to get his XDJ system to allow him to hamster scratch. So I changed his setup to allow him to reverse the crossfader, which hasn't been automatically allowed through a firmware update in his system."

"Is that why he let you choose your own songs?" Zoe asked.

Dot shot her a grin. "You know it. I've always wanted to be a DJ. Maybe in another life."

"We're going to need another life when that bouncer sees us," I muttered as we reached the door. "Ready to run?" I asked Zoe, who had already taken her heels off.

"I'm glad I'm up to date on my tetanus shots," she replied with a nod, holding up the shoes.

"We'll see you tomorrow," Rosie said. "You make a run for it. Dot and I will distract the bouncer."

"Thanks," I said, shooting them both a smile. "I'll see you tomorrow, I guess, since it turns out this case isn't actually solved yet."

"Now I'm extra curious as to who did it," Dot said. "Because not only did they murder Jo, but they had the presence of mind to try and frame someone else for it too."

"Okay, here we go," Zoe said as we reached the door. She opened it, and the two of us quickly speed-walked back toward the car.

"Hey!" the bouncer called after us.

But then I heard Dot's voice. "Excuse me, sir, but do you think this looks infected?"

The gagging sound the bouncer made confirmed that he no longer really cared about Zoe and me, and I snickered as the two of us darted back toward our car.

"So that settles it," I said as we drove off. "We learned a lot tonight. First of all, we're too old to be let into the sketchy clubs with cradle robbers, and secondly, Sean Sherman couldn't have killed Jo Lismore."

"That sounds about right," Zoe replied with a laugh. "I for one am glad to leave my clubbing days behind me. It's almost eleven. It's past my bedtime."

"Should I take a detour to the nearest nursing home and drop you off?" I asked with a grin.

"Ask me again in a couple of hours. I do like this Jeep. It's nice to have the wind flowing through my hair. How old is it?"

"A ninety-three."

"Hmm, almost the same vintage as we are. It runs really well for its age."

"Yeah. Olivia, the woman who sold it to me and who runs a garage, seems to really know what she's doing."

"Cool. I'm going to suffer tomorrow; my shift starts at six. Why do I let you talk me into these things?"

I grinned. "Because whenever you go out with me, we always have a ton of fun?"

"That's a weird way of pronouncing 'committing felonies.'"

"Po-tay-toh, po-tah-to."

Zoe shook her head at me. "Well, I'm glad we didn't get arrested, at least. How do you do this regularly? I'm pretty sure I aged at least five years tonight."

"What? You work in an emergency room where people come in with bullet wounds and heart attacks and everything in between, and if you don't react in time, they die. That's so much worse than what we did tonight."

"At least being a doctor is legal."

"Well, it is if *you* do it."

Zoe shot me a look. "You know what I mean. I don't think I've ever had so much adrenaline course through my body at once. And I'm glad the cops weren't called."

"Don't worry, I'm pretty sure a place like The Horny Turtle has seen a lot worse than two almost-thirty-year-olds try and sneak in. That probably isn't even going to make the top one hundred list of weird things that's happened here this week."

"That's true," Zoe snorted. "Anyway, I'm crashing. Thanks for the adventure. Try not to get arrested anytime soon."

"I'll do my best."

"Or Tasered," she added with a yawn as she headed down the hall to her bedroom.

I FOLLOWED SOON AFTERWARD—AND AS I SANK DEEP into the new memory-foam mattress Zoe had ordered, I silently thanked her for being so, so much more organized than me. I'd probably have been sleeping on the couch for at least a month before I'd have gotten around to buying a mattress if I'd been on my own.

The next morning, I was heading out to work when I ran into a little girl, probably somewhere between seven and ten years old. I wasn't exactly great at aging kids. Her light-brown hair was braided on either side of her head, and she sat in the hallway, her backpack sitting next to her, reading a book pressed against her legs.

"You're the new neighbor," she said matter-of-factly. "Charlie. Right?"

I had to admit I was a bit taken aback. "Yeah."

"I'm Frances. But you can call me Franny." She stood up and held out a hand to shake as if this was a business meeting.

"Nice to meet you, Franny. Do you live in this building as well?"

She nodded. "Yeah. Me and my dad live in number 10."

"What are you reading?"

"The latest *Harriet the Spy* book."

"Is it good?"

Franny shrugged. "It's all right. It's a little bit young for me, I think. I want to read *real* spy books, but Dad doesn't think it's a good idea. And they don't carry *Tinker Tailor Soldier Spy* at my school library."

I raised an eyebrow at this obviously precocious child. "Is that how you knew my name? You've been spying on me?"

"Some people call it spying, but I think it's just paying attention to things. For example, I heard you speaking with the policeman, Jake, yesterday. I recognize your voice, and he called you that. So I know your name."

Just then, a man came out of the apartment down the hall. He shot me an apologetic look. "I'm sorry. I hope Franny hasn't been bothering you."

"Not at all," I said with a smile. "She's great."

"I am," Franny confirmed.

I laughed.

"I'm Frank, her father," the man said, shaking my hand. He looked a little bit run-down, with bags under his eyes and his black shirt on inside out. "It's nice to meet you."

"Dad, your shirt's on inside out," Franny pointed out, and I bit back a smile as Frank looked down, muttering a curse word under his breath so Franny couldn't hear.

"I'll be right back," he said, rushing back into his apartment.

"Dad isn't very good at time management," Franny told me with an apologetic look I would have expected from someone twenty years her senior. "But it's okay, and not entirely his fault. I set the clocks in the apartment back fifteen minutes, so we always end up being late for school."

I laughed despite myself. "Not a fan of school?"

Franny shook her head. "It's all quite boring, really. And the other kids take so long to learn anything. It's all right, though. I get to read my books that way."

Frank rushed back out. "Okay, Franny. We have to get going." He flashed me a smile. "Hopefully we'll catch up some other time, but we're running late today."

"No problem at all. You know where to find me."

Frank took Franny by the hand and walked down the hall with her. Franny still held her book in her other hand, but she looked behind her and waved at me with it.

I waved back. Franny was a weird kid, but I liked her.

Chapter 22

When I entered Aloha Ice Cream that morning, Leslie was in a somber mood. "I was thinking of closing at noon. I want us to be able to go to Jo's funeral."

"That's very good of you."

"Have you found out who did it yet?"

"I have some good leads."

"I'm glad to hear it. Between you and the police, I want that killer found."

"You and me both. Can I take off if we're closing early? I want to speak with Randall."

"Of course."

"Thanks. Sorry for constantly running out on you like this."

Leslie waved away my apology. "It's low season. I can handle it. And besides, you're doing a good thing."

"I'll see you at the funeral."

I flashed her a quick smile and headed out the

door. I wanted to speak to Randall before the funeral. After all, I'd told him on the phone last night that we'd likely found his daughter's killer, and I needed to tell him before the funeral started that I had been wrong.

I gave Randall a call as I walked to the car. "Charlie, how are you?" he asked.

"Okay. Listen, I need to talk to you."

"I'm at the business. Come down whenever."

"Great. I'll be there in twenty."

I hung up the phone and bit my lip. This wasn't going to be a pleasant conversation, but it had to happen. I had messed up.

I spent the whole drive over there thinking about the case. It didn't make any sense. Sean Sherman had had the gun in his apartment. He'd just been fired by Jo, who was his dealer. So who had framed him?

Thoughts tumbled in my mind until I reached the business once more. Natalie pursed her lips when she saw me. "Still haven't solved this thing, huh? I can't say I'm surprised. You were never the brightest shade of lipstick in the bag. Even after all the help I gave you."

I snorted. "Please. Sure, you let me know Jo was dealing. Wow, I never would have figured that out without you. Oh wait, I forgot—I found a ton of Percocet in her apartment."

Natalie glared at me. "You know what? I shouldn't have helped you at all."

"Please, like you were doing it for me. You're worried the killer works here, and you don't want to be next. Anyway, I'm meeting Randall."

"Yeah, he said you'd be in. Let me take you to his office."

Natalie stood up and walked toward the main work area without another word. I followed her up to the mezzanine and to an office at the back. She knocked twice then opened the door.

"Randall, Charlotte Gibson is here to see you about poor Jo's unsolved murder." Natalie gave me a smug look as she turned and started walking back toward the reception area.

"At least I've solved the mystery of how to find a hairdresser who knows what they're doing," I muttered back as she walked past, loud enough for only her to hear. She glared at me but didn't dare respond with her boss right there. Instead, Natalie left, and I found myself facing Randall.

"What is it?" he asked.

"Sean Sherman didn't kill your daughter," I replied. I figured it was best to get it right out there straight away.

"Are you sure?" Randall replied.

"Yes. He has an alibi. The gun that was found in his apartment is the one that killed her, though. I'm sorry. I wanted you to know before the funeral."

Randall closed his eyes and took a breath before replying. "Thank you for telling me. I appreciate that you didn't simply find the gun and call it a day."

I nodded. "I'll do right by Jo as best I can. How much do you know about Sean Sherman?"

"Not much. I'd say hi to him, of course. But he was about three rungs down the ladder from me, so I didn't have much to do with him day to day. You'd be better off speaking to Jo's direct boss, Jonathan. Or his coworkers."

"Thanks. If you don't mind, I'll have another chat with them."

"Of course. What does any of this matter? I don't care about this company anymore. I devoted my entire life to it, to build something for my family, to build something for Jo. And now…" Randall sighed as he trailed off, his eyes falling to his desk. "Yes, speak with whoever you want."

"Thank you."

"Will you be at the funeral today?"

I nodded. "Yes."

"Thank you. Jo was special. She wasn't perfect; I know that. Nobody is perfect. Not being perfect doesn't mean you deserve to be killed, though."

"I agree completely."

"I'll see you later this afternoon, then."

I nodded and left Randall's office, heading back down the stairs to the open area.

I found Jonathan working at his desk and grabbed a nearby empty chair, flipping it around and sitting in it so the chair's back covered my chest. It didn't help. Seriously, did Jonathan think he had X-ray vision or something?

"Hi," he said to the chair. "Back for more information?"

"Yes. I'm wondering what you can tell me about Sean Sherman, who worked here."

"Not much, I'm afraid. He worked under Jo, I

know that, and he was the first employee she ever had to fire. I can tell you she was broken up about it. She came to me for advice on how to do it. You know, what with my experience in the business side of things."

"She wasn't confident?"

"No. Of course, no one ever is the first time they need to fire somebody. It's not easy."

"Did she tell you why she was firing him?"

"Oh, that was easy. He wasn't showing up for work, and when he did show up, his work was awful. Jo showed me some of it; she was one hundred percent correct in making that decision."

"Was there anyone here who disliked him? Maybe pushed for him to be fired?"

"I'm afraid I'm not really sure. As I said, I didn't work directly with Jo's team very often; I was always more on the management side of things. But you know, you may want to speak with Evan. I believe he always had issues with Sean."

"You're sure there's no one else who disliked him here?" Evan had a rock-solid alibi; he couldn't have killed Jo. Katrina had backed him up, and seeing as he'd paid her for the privilege of spending the night, I was inclined to believe her. She wasn't going to risk going to jail for a client by lying about his whereabouts when someone was murdered.

Jonathan shrugged. "I imagine there was resentment. Most people don't particularly enjoy it when their coworkers get away with slacking off and they have to work harder to compensate. But he was fired, so I bet that was the end of it. Beyond that, I don't know of any particular disputes."

"Okay, thanks," I said. That was disappointing. I left the building, thinking that I was probably on the wrong track, anyway. The murder had probably had something to do with the drugs Jo had been dealing and not her work. I mean, statistically, that was *far* more likely.

I wondered briefly if Phil McCracken was going to be at the funeral. What was the etiquette for a drug distributor to his supplier? Did it count as a regular employer–employee relationship? I'd never really had to consider it before. I supposed I was going to find out.

HO'OLEWA MORTUARY WAS LOCATED ONLY A FEW blocks from the hospital. I supposed it saved on travel cost. The red-brick exterior with a stone façade, combined with the striped, sun-faded awnings, made me think this had probably been an Applebee's at some point before being transformed into something slightly more depressing.

I took a deep breath before entering. The last time I'd been here had been at my own father's funeral, and I wasn't entirely ready for the flood of emotions that hit me as I stepped past the threshold.

Greeting me was the owner, Bradley Rudolph, who surely couldn't be much longer for this world himself. He had been old when Dad died, and now he was straight-up ancient. He was still around six feet tall, with just a few wisps of white hair dotting the top of his head, and wearing a dark three-piece suit. Liver spots dotted his face, and his blue eyes had gone quite a bit paler than the last time I had seen Bradley. Still, he kept the same expression of deep-set sympathy he'd been practicing for the twenty or so years that he'd owned this place.

"Welcome," he murmured, taking my hand in both of his as I entered. "Please accept my deepest sympathies for your loss. Jo's funeral will be taking place in the Eternal Rest room on the left."

"Thank you," I said, flashing him a small smile quickly and doing my best to get as far away from him as fast as I could. I really wasn't comfortable here at all.

I headed down the narrow hallway that split into two rooms, one on either side of the building. Eternal Rest and Forever Free. The interior of the Eternal Rest room was already fairly packed. I scanned the room, looking for familiar faces, especially that of Phil McCracken. I had to talk to him.

Instead, I spotted Leslie almost straight away, standing against the wall to my left, her expression stoic. Randall and Heather were at the front of the room, next to a gold-and-mahogany coffin nearly completely covered with hibiscus flowers in all shades. In the center stood an enormous framed photo of Jo, smiling away as she stood on the bow of a boat, squinting against the sun in her eyes.

Casey sat about three rows from the front, crying

into a tissue. There was no sign of Phil. I headed to a corner of the room and did my best to blend in with the plastic plants. If he arrived, I didn't want to scare him off.

He ended up walking in about a minute before the funeral began. I pressed myself closer against the wall, but he went the other way, standing at the back of the room as well.

When the ceremony finished, I kept an eye on him. I wanted to know why Phil was here. It wasn't as if he was especially broken up by Jo's death. Even if you factored in his fear when he'd been kidnapped by Dot and Rosie and the three of us had interrogated him, he only seemed to care about the money and not Jo herself.

That was why, as he walked up and joined the line of mourners, I followed closely behind him. He reached Randall and shook his hand then leaned in close behind him. As soon as I saw Randall's eyes widen, I knew Phil was up to something.

I grabbed him by the arm, hard, and he turned to me, a shocked expression on his face.

"What the hell are you doing here?"

"Stopping you from being an ass at a freaking funeral," I hissed. "Now, you can either come with me quietly, or we can do this the loud way. And you know how the loud way ended for you last time. I promise you, if you mess up this funeral for Jo's family, I will make sure it ends worse for you."

"Okay, okay, I'm coming," Phil complained.

I yanked his arm hard, pulling him out of the line.

Randall, for his part, looked a bit stunned and confused.

"What did you say to Randall just then?" I asked when we were outside in the parking lot.

"Nothing," Phil replied with a shrug. "I just told him how much money his daughter owed me and that I expected to get it back from him."

"Right. Did you tell him *why* she owed you?"

"No. I'm not a monster." Phil looked around uneasily. "Are those two old ladies here with you?"

"Yes, but they're staying out of sight. I suggest you answer my questions. You just thought you'd accost the man at his own daughter's funeral?"

"Hey, I'm a pragmatist. He wasn't going to make a scene there, especially with his wife right next to him. I bet neither one of them know about the dealing. It was just a good opportunity. You can't blame me for wanting my money. I have to pay a supplier too. I need that money. They're going to kill me if I don't pay them, and I have no product or cash for them."

"I mean, isn't that a cost of doing business? You've got to get ripped off a lot."

"Just because we commit drug offenses doesn't mean we're also thieves. That's prejudicial and insulting." Phil crossed his arms in front of him, obviously annoyed.

"Right, sorry for mixing up what felonies you actually commit," I replied.

"Anyway, twenty grand isn't petty cash. I need that money."

"There are kinder ways than doing that by accosting the family at a funeral."

Phil shrugged. "If I went to his office, I'd be kicked out in an instant. And the cops would be called."

"Okay, well, help me find who killed her. Do you know Sean Sherman?"

"Sure. Lowlife from the island. Jo was his dealer."

"Did you have anything against him?"

"Nope. He was a good customer from what I heard and never asked for credit. That's always a bad sign, when customers start asking for stuff without paying."

"So you wouldn't have any reason to frame him for murder?"

Phil looked genuinely shocked. "Me? No, of course not."

"Who do you think might have? And think *hard*, Phil. Because what you say will impact whether I'm going to let you go or whether I'm going to tell the cops everything I know about you."

"Look, look, I don't know, okay? I really don't."

"That doesn't sound like you're thinking very hard."

"Fine, hold on." Phil put his hands on his knees, taking a couple deep breaths. I wouldn't have been surprised if he'd taken something before coming to the funeral. "Okay, I'm thinking. Sean Sherman. Sean. I've seen him at clubs and stuff."

"The Horny Turtle?"

"Yeah. That's the kind of place he likes to hang out. Plus, there's so much stupid stuff that goes on over there that they don't really pay attention if you're doing drugs, as long as you're not being super obvious about it."

"Okay. Who do you know who has a problem with him?"

Phil ran a hand down his face. "He was having issues at work. I know that."

"Yeah, he got fired. That counts as an issue."

"Jo fired him, right? Well, I'd say he had an issue with that."

"Yes, thanks for pointing out the obvious. Who else?"

"Did Sean not kill Jo?"

I shook my head. "He has a rock-solid alibi, and someone framed him for it. So unless you want me to start looking even more closely at you, I suggest you think real hard."

"You're joking. Who would frame someone like that?"

"That's what I'm asking you." People who were high were the worst. It was like talking to a brick wall. Plus it was not as if Phil was a MENSA candidate to begin with. "Can you at the very least point me to one of his friends? Someone who might know a little bit more than you?"

"Yeah. I can do that, yeah. For sure. Talk to Dan Jessup. I'm pretty sure he's friends with Sean."

"Where can I find Dan?"

"They worked together. Or at the same company, at least. I don't know what Dan did there, but it was different from Sean."

"Great. Thanks."

"Does this mean you're going to let me go?"

"This means you're going to get into my Jeep, and we're going to take a ride so I can make sure you're not going to keep bothering the nice family at a funeral."

Horror was etched all over Phil's face. "You're not going to take me to Wailua Falls, are you?"

"What? No, of course not. Why would I drive all the way over there?"

"That's what those two crazy old ladies did when they kidnapped me. They drove me to the falls, took my clothes, and left me there. I had to take some Maui queen leaves off a plant to cover myself. I thought the first old people to show up were going to call the cops."

I burst out laughing. Wailua Falls was in the middle of the ever-popular road to Hana. There was no way Phil could have gotten back without a ride. "I didn't know that was what they did."

"Yeah. They're insane. Who *does* that to someone?"

"I dunno. You Tasered me. I could ask you the same thing."

"That was an accident. Luckily, a group of guys from Texas came by after a few hours. One of them had an extra change of clothes, and they drove me back to town. I told them my girlfriend broke up with me. It was easier than the truth and less embarrassing."

"Did they believe you?"

"I think so. Though I'm pretty sure one of them didn't and thought it was just a weird sex thing."

I grinned. "At least you didn't get arrested."

"No. I bet that's what your crazy friends wanted, though."

"I imagine they just wanted you to be as embarrassed as possible."

"Well, it worked. Have you ever had to hide naked in the woods for hours and then beg for a ride?"

"No," I said. "But then, I've never tried to drive someone off the road, either."

Phil scowled. "I told you, I needed those drugs."

"The second part I believe. Now, get in."

Phil climbed into Queenie's passenger seat. I grabbed some zip ties out of the back, and as soon as he saw them, he started whining. "Oh, come on. You don't have to do that. I promise I'll be good."

"I don't exactly have great experiences with you and a car. So yeah, I'm zip-tying your hands together."

I had no idea where these had even come from. I assumed Rosie had left them behind at some point.

"Fine," Phil said, looking through the rearview mirror. He was obviously still petrified that Dot and Rosie were going to come out of the bushes and ambush him again. I couldn't believe they had stolen his clothes and left him by the highway. That was hilarious.

Chapter 23

I was much kinder than Dot and Rosie had been and dropped Phil off in downtown Kihei. He was far enough away that he wouldn't be able to get back to the funeral before it ended, but he'd also be able to get a ride wherever he needed to go reasonably easily.

Meanwhile, I immediately turned the car around and headed back to Jo's place of work. I needed to talk to Dan.

Natalie scowled as soon as she saw me. "You again?"

"Yeah, believe it or not, some of us actually work for a living instead of just playing on our phones all day."

"I do work. It's not my fault this place doesn't have a stream of people coming through. Well, apart from you."

I rolled my eyes. "Dan Jessup. I was told he works here; I need to talk to him."

"Fine." Natalie rolled back her chair and heaved

herself upward as if it was the biggest inconvenience in her life to have to help me. She walked back toward the offices. I followed her to the desk of a man who looked to be in his mid-twenties. Frankly, given what I knew about Sean, Dan looked surprisingly well put together. He obviously worked out but not so much that his arms looked like a loaf of well-cooked challah bread. His light-brown hair was short, he was clean-shaven, and he tapped diligently away at the computer keyboard. He was pretty hot, I had to say.

"Hey, Dan," Natalie said sweetly as she reached his desk. It didn't take a genius to know she was into him. She leaned seductively against his desk, biting her lower lip. "This is Charlie. She's looking into Jo's death, which was *such* a tragedy. We all loved her so much. Can you please give her a hand with whatever she needs? I'd appreciate it. And you know, just be patient with her. *She's a little slow.*"

Natalie whispered that last part but loudly enough that I was obviously intended to hear it. I rolled my eyes. Obviously, Natalie hadn't learned anything from her complete failure at bullying me when we were kids.

"Sure," Dan said casually, looking over and flashing me a friendly smile. He completely ignored her jab.

"You're *such* a doll for doing this, Dan. Really, it shows how good a heart you have."

"Thanks, Natalie," I said, flashing her my friend-liest smile. "I really appreciate it. Good luck with those hemorrhoids you were telling me about. I hope the new, stronger meds your doctor gave you work this time."

Natalie's face went beet red as she looked from me to Dan and then back to me. "I do not have hemorrhoids," she screeched, her voice echoing across the room.

Every face in the office turned to Natalie and she clasped her hand against her mouth as she realized what had happened.

Next to me, Dan snorted, masking it with a cough —badly.

Natalie glared at me. "You ruin everything!" Then she stormed off.

What could I say? She'd started it.

I turned to Dan and held out a hand, which he shook. "Nice to meet you."

"You too. Although I'm not sure how I can help you. I didn't know Jo beyond to say hi to."

"I'm actually here to talk about Sean Sherman. I heard the two of you were friends."

"Uh, yeah. We were. Hey, I'm due a break. Mind if I go grab some food while we chat? There's a burger place just down the street."

"Sure," I said with a nod.

Dan got up, and the two of us headed back out the front. I stuck my tongue out at Natalie on the way, and she replied by flipping me off, which just made me laugh. All these years, and she still never learned that it was impossible to bully me because I just didn't care about her opinion.

A few minutes later, we were seated in a plastic

booth by the window. Dan had a plastic tray in front of him with a burger and fries. I ended up ordering a cheeseburger and fries myself; it turned out I hadn't eaten all day, and my stomach began to rumble as soon as the familiar scent of overcooked grease reached my nostrils.

"So, you're friends with Sean?"

"Yeah. I mean, as much as anybody could be, I guess. He's in the hospital right now."

"I know. I was the one who found him."

"Oh. Thanks for getting him medical attention. Sean… Sean has problems, but he's not a bad guy. He didn't deserve to die because he's an addict."

"So you know about the pills."

Dan nodded. "Sure."

"How long has he been using?"

"About six months. He was in a car accident that mangled his leg pretty badly. He was on painkillers for that, and he got hooked. When his doctor realized what was going on, he refused to continue writing prescriptions for Sean, and he had to go elsewhere."

"The black market."

"Yup. Jo was his supplier."

"You knew about that?"

"Everyone in the office knew. Well, apart from her dad. No one would have ever dared to tell him that his perfect daughter was into something like that."

"He wouldn't have taken it well?"

"Randall liked to think Jo was going to take over for him. She didn't seem especially interested in it as far as I could tell. I mean, sure, she did a good job at work, but it's not like she was scrambling to front the company."

"So, there was a bit of a disconnect there?"

"A big one. Of course, it wasn't entirely his fault. He had blinders on to some extent when it came to his daughter, but she always put on a good show whenever he was around."

"Okay. So, what did she want to do with her life?"

"Wouldn't have a clue."

"What about Sean? You say the whole office knew she was supplying him with drugs. Do you know of any troubles the two of them were having? I heard he didn't take it well when he got fired."

"No, he didn't. I told him he deserved it, though. And he did. He let the drugs take over his life. I get it, addiction is a disease, blah, blah, blah, all of that. But Sean had to take some responsibility too. He didn't care. He loved how he felt on the drugs, so he kept taking them. I warned him he was getting noticed at work. Or more accurately, he *wasn't* being noticed at work, because he wasn't there. He ended up getting fired. I feel bad for him and all, but I mean, what can you do? There's only so much help I can offer. The rest was on him."

"Do you know of anyone else who had issues with Sean? Someone who might have hated him? Especially at work."

Dan shook his head. "No. Generally, Sean is non-confrontational. He could get a little bit aggressive when he had a bit of alcohol in him, and he's been in a couple of bar fights, but that's it. When it comes to work, no one had any issues with him beyond the fact that he stopped showing up to work, and that when he did, the work was crap. But he got fired, and as far as I know, any resentment from others ended there."

"Did he mention keeping in touch with anyone after he was fired?"

"No. He was a quiet guy, generally. At least, when he was sober, and it's not like he ever showed up to work plastered, for all his faults. So he never had any run-ins with anyone, but he also didn't really have a lot of friends. I'm pretty sure I was the only one."

I blew air upwards into my bangs. This wasn't helping, but I was also pretty sure Dan was telling the truth. "Did you meet Sean at work?"

"No, we met in college. He got me this job, actually. I'm not a programmer—a computer toucher, as the guys like to say—but I work on the finance side of things."

"The company's doing well?"

"Sure. I can't get into specifics without Randall's permission, obviously, but let's just say it's not struggling. If you're trying to find a motive for Jo's death, it's not there."

"Okay. Thanks."

I was just getting ready to open my mouth to ask another question when the window next to me exploded.

I instinctively fell to the side onto the plastic booth, covering my head as shards of glass rained down on me. Rolling under the table for protection, I looked over to see Dan next to me, surprise etched all over his face.

Screams pierced the air inside the restaurant. Outside, tires screeched and horns beeped.

"What the hell was that?" he asked.

I shook my head. I had absolutely no idea. I carefully peeked out to make sure there wasn't some sort of crazed gunman coming after me. After all, I didn't plan on dying on the floor of a fast-food joint. If someone was coming for me, I was going to fight. Even if all I had to fight with was half a cheeseburger.

All I saw as I carefully peered through the frame of the broken window, however, were shocked-looking bystanders. I gingerly stepped from the bench over the window frame and onto the lawn outside the restaurant, homing in on a couple of teenage boys who had been walking toward the restaurant. Now they looked at the damage, stunned expressions all over their faces.

"Hey, guys," I said to them. "Did you see who did this, by chance?"

"Uh, yeah," one of them replied, running a hand through his short brown hair. "It was crazy. Some dude. He had a Yankees cap on and a bandana over his face."

"You couldn't make out who he was?"

"Only that it was a guy," another one of the teenagers offered. "He had jeans on and a hoodie. It was, like, black with a yellow Batman symbol on it or something. Can't tell you more than that. Sorry."

"The gun was a Walther PPK, if that helps," the

third kid said. He was the shortest of the three, with blond curls.

"What the hell? How would you know that? The only guns you've ever seen are playing *Fortnite*," the first guy said.

"Yeah, well, I watch a lot of James Bond movies," the other kid shot back. "You're just jealous because I actually recognized the gun."

"Damn, I watch James Bond movies too. How come I didn't recognize it?"

"You don't pay enough attention, obviously," the blond kid said to his friend with a grin.

"Whatever, Fred."

"Okay, can you guys tell me what happened?"

"He came from there," the first kid said, pointing to the west. "He was just walking along the sidewalk, like a normal guy, and I didn't even notice the bandana until the last second. Then he, like, stopped, looked into the restaurant window for a second, then pulled the gun out from his hoodie. He shot at you, three times, I think, then ran right past us and back that way. One of the cars slammed on the brakes to avoid hitting him. He was only a few feet away from us."

"I was so shocked I didn't even think to stop him," the middle kid said, shaking his head. "It was crazy. Never seen anything like it."

"Do you think they're still making burgers with the broken window? I don't want to have to walk down to the Burger King," the blond guy whined.

I bit back a smile. Teenagers never changed. "Wait, you're sure he shot at me?" I asked.

Fred nodded. "Yeah. He stopped, looked in the direction of the window, then moved his head forward like he was squinting for a better look, you know? Then he kind of nodded to himself, pulled out the gun, and pointed it right at you."

"Cool. Thanks, guys," I told them, my stomach churning.

I turned and carefully climbed back through the window, brushed glass from the bench, and sat down at the table. I looked longingly at my abandoned cheeseburger, but shards of glass stuck out from the bun. Besides, I was pretty sure I'd just lost my appetite.

"Someone just shot at us," Dan said.

"Correction: someone just shot at *me*. You were just unlucky enough to be at the same table."

Dan gaped. "Who would shoot you?"

"My best guess is the person who killed Jo. And at this point, at least I can narrow the gender down to male."

"It was a guy?"

I nodded. "So say the teenagers outside who saw it all go down."

"What do we do now?"

"We wait for the cops, I guess."

Chapter 24

J ake and Liam walked in about five minutes later. His eyes scanned the scene and landed on me. He paused, closed his eyes for a second, took a deep breath, and walked over toward me. Liam, for his part, scowled and purposely headed in the opposite direction. That was more than fine with me.

"How come every time I get called to a crime scene, you're somehow involved?"

"Well, if it makes you feel better, I didn't shoot the window out myself."

"She didn't," Dan confirmed.

"Thanks," Jake replied with a wry smile. "So, is this… a date?"

"Yup," I said quickly. "Dan here's my new boyfriend."

"Really?" Jake asked, his eyes narrowing slightly. "And he brought you here… on a date?"

"His work is just around the corner. It's convenient."

"Let me guess: your *date* works for Randall Lismore's company."

I flashed Jake a fake smile. "How did you guess?"

He glared at me in return. "I told you to stop investigating this case."

"Haven't you got it all wrapped up? Didn't you arrest Sean Sherman for the crime?"

"The fact that you're here speaking with Dan— don't think for a minute that I believe this whole 'date' stuff—means you know Sean didn't do it. We released him this morning."

"You found the video on his phone too, huh?"

"I'm more interested in how you found it."

"Really? Because if I were you, I'd be more interested in finding out who just tried to shoot me. But then, I have a bit more of a personal stake in that one."

"I can ask about two things at once, you know."

"That's funny, because so far, you've only asked about whether I'm still looking for the person who killed Jo and not about the person who just actually tried to kill me."

"Err, do you two want to be alone?" Dan asked, a small smile flittering onto his lips.

Jake pursed his lips, shaking his head. "Not necessary. Can you tell me what happened?"

"We were just sitting here, talking," Dan said. "Then the window exploded."

I nodded in agreement. "Yeah. I went and talked to those kids out there. They said he was walking along, looked into the window, saw me, pulled out a

Walther PPK, shot at me a few times, then ran past them and out of sight. I guess everyone was too stunned to do anything."

"A Walther PPK, huh?"

I shrugged. "One of the kids is way too into James Bond movies."

"Hey, if being a James Bond nerd gets me a gun identified, I'll take it."

"Fair enough. That's all I know, anyway."

"Neither one of you were hit?"

I shook my head. "As far as I know, all the bullets went wide."

"Good. Okay, stay here. I'm probably going to want to speak to you again before this is all over. Neither one of you need medical attention?"

We both shook our heads, and Dan held out an arm. "I've got a bit of a cut here, but it's nothing some gauze and Polysporin won't fix. I'm fine."

"All right," Jake said. "Thanks for hanging out. I'm going to see what I can find about the person who did this."

I watched with rapt attention from my spot on the bench as Jake moved around the crime scene, deftly interviewing other patrons and employees. He went outside and had a chat with the teenagers, as well as a young family who had stayed behind. A driver who had pulled over handed him a flash card; obviously there was a chance at some dash cam footage.

It was looking like there was a chance that whoever had shot at me might actually be caught.

And I had a sneaking suspicion whoever that was

had also killed Jo. After all, who else on this island would want to kill me? Not even Natalie hated me *that* much.

About half an hour later, Jake returned to our table. He took down Dan's contact information and sent him on his way then sat across from me.

"So you knew Sean Sherman hadn't done it?"

I nodded. "Yeah. We found the video footage from the Horny Turtle."

"And you didn't feel the need to tell me about it?"

I shrugged. "I figured you'd get there on your own. I mean, if it came to it, I wasn't going to let Sean go to trial or anything without handing the footage over. But seeing as you keep telling me to keep my nose out of it, I figured you wouldn't have taken it well if I'd told you about it."

Jake sighed. "You're really not going to let this go, are you?"

"I've been hired to do a job, and I'm going to do it."

"Really? Still? Even after someone shot at you?"

"I mean, it's not ideal. Would I rather this not have happened? Of course. Am I probably going to go home and drink an entire bottle of wine to pretend that my legs aren't trembling under the table? Yeah. Am I going to stay up all night with a baseball bat in front of my apartment? Also yes. But how is the person who just tried to kill me going to know if I've given up on the case? They're not. So I might as well try and find them before they try and find me."

"Or you could—and I'm just spitballing here—leave it to the police."

"Right. Just the way you've found Jo's killer."

Jake sighed. "I'm serious, Charlie. As much as you're infuriating—and I swear I'm going to have to mention you to my doctor when I go for a checkup and he asks why my blood pressure is so high—I don't want to see you get hurt."

"Believe it or not, that's up there on my desires in life too."

"And yet everything you do seems to go against that."

"That's not true. Up until about an hour ago, I was just doing another job. I had no idea someone wanted to kill me."

"Okay. Well, I can tell this conversation is going nowhere, and I have a bullet I have to get to the lab."

"You found one of them?"

Jake nodded. "Wedged in the menu. Apparently, the shooter isn't a big fan of apple pies."

I smiled despite myself. "Was the blond kid right? Was it a Walther PPK?"

"Well, I don't know about that, but the caliber is right for it. There can't be *that* many registered guns of that make on the island, so I'll take a look at the list."

"Okay. Can you let me know if you find anything?"

Jake shot me a look that said he'd rather eat a toothpaste sandwich, and I figured it was time to make my exit.

"All right, thanks for looking into this, anyway."

"I'll be in touch. It's not like I don't know where to find you."

"Right."

I headed back up the street to where I'd left Queenie and drove right on over to Dot's apartment, making a quick stop along the way.

"Oh, honey, if you're here for the reason I think you're here, that wine isn't going to cut it," Dot said when she opened the door, grabbing the couple bottles from my hand as she motioned for me to enter.

"And what do you think that is?"

"You were at the restaurant that just got shot up, weren't you?"

"How could you *possibly* know that?"

"You look like you've seen a ghost, for one thing. Secondly, this is Maui. Violent crime isn't exactly a regular occurrence here, so it's not a stretch to think it's linked to the murder. And thirdly, you were three blocks away from where Jo worked."

"Well, you're three for three," I said.

Dot headed into her kitchen. She opened a cabinet and grabbed a bottle of Johnnie Walker Blue. She poured a generous three fingers into a glass.

I took it and downed the whole thing in a single gulp, the elixir burning as it went down my throat. "Someone shot at me while I was interviewing Sean Sherman's best friend."

"Did you find out who did it?" Dot grabbed my glass and poured me a bit more scotch.

While I was tempted to repeat the same maneuver I'd made with the last, I forced myself to take a small sip this time, ignoring the fact that my hands shook slightly. I shook my head. "It all happened too fast. I think everyone was stunned. All I know is it was a male, using a Walther PPK, dressed in jeans and a hoodie, covering his face with a bandana."

"So you've narrowed it down to half the population of the island."

"Essentially," I said with a shrug. "I'm afraid I don't know anything beyond that."

"Well, that's too bad. It could have been a good opportunity to catch the bastard."

"I'm guessing that means you think it was Jo's killer too?"

"Obviously. You have a bit of a mouth on you, but if someone was going to murder you for that, they wouldn't premeditate it. They'd be more likely to pull out a knife on the spot and stab you or something."

"That's a reassuring thought. I agree with you, though. I think Jo's killer is trying to get rid of me."

"Do you have any idea who it is?"

"Not yet. I certainly don't think it was Phil. He's terrified of you, by the way. Did you really leave him naked in the woods halfway to Hana?"

"We sure did," Dot replied with an impish grin. "How did you find him?"

"He was at Jo's funeral. He decided that was an appropriate time to try and get his money back, so I decided it was an appropriate time to escort him off the property and find out who Sean's friends were."

"Did you get anywhere?"

I shrugged. "Sort of. I spoke to Dan, his best friend

from work, but he didn't seem to know who would have framed Sean. It sounds like Sean was the keep-to-himself sort."

"I wish he applied that rule to his wiener."

"Ugh, me too. It sounds like he could be an aggressive drunk, but he was never drunk at work."

"Okay," Dot said. "So, do you think you were followed?"

I nodded. "That makes the most sense. He wouldn't have been able to get into the business—though I'm sure Natalie would have rolled the red carpet out for him if he told her what he was going to do—so he waited for me to leave, followed us, and then took his shot while we were eating."

"I just wish you had more to go on as to his identification."

"Me too. I didn't see him at all. I was too busy shielding myself from the glass raining down on me."

"Well, you won't find me arguing with that. Rosie might, but then Rosie probably would have picked up that she was being followed."

"Yeah, she'll probably comment on my car and how I need something a little bit more subtle."

Dot snorted. "Most likely. What's your plan now?"

I shrugged. "Honestly? Haven't got one. I was going to go home and keep drinking."

"Not after that much scotch, you're not."

"Hey, that's your fault. I just brought over wine."

"Yeah, two bottles of it. And I'm sure you intended to drink a whole one. I'll drive you home when Rosie comes over here, but she's at the grocery store right now."

"I should text her to pick up snacks," I said, taking my glass and walking over to the lanai. I plonked myself down on a lounger while Dot poured herself a glass of the scotch and joined me, bringing the bottle over with her. She turned on the fan, and I closed my eyes, letting the warm, humid Maui air wash over me.

I took another sip, the effects of the alcohol from the first shot just starting to take effect. My tongue loosened slightly, and I felt just a tiny bit lightheaded. It was a nice feeling. "So, is this how the superhacker lives?" I asked. "Scotch that's smooth as silk, a computer that knows everything, and tons of books on true crime?"

Dot grinned. "That's my life, and I wish I'd started it a lot earlier."

"You mean you weren't teaching high school kids how to bury bodies when you worked as a librarian?"

"No, the administration frowns on that sort of thing. Although I could be subversive in my own way."

"I feel like there's a story there."

Dot grinned. "The school I worked at had a very long list of books we weren't supposed to order. I would just so happen to buy those books myself, and somehow, they'd end up on our shelves. Luckily, the principal wasn't exactly what you would call a reader, and only one parent complained in all the years I taught. I claimed that I had no idea how the book had gotten there, that it must have been a prank by a kid who graduated years ago, and that was that. That was my form of rebellion as a younger adult. Rosie was the one of the two of us who always knew what she was doing. I just stumbled into it later in life."

I leaned on my arm to get a better look at her. "You? Really? I had the impression that you were always this way."

Dot smiled at me before looking into her glass and downing it in a single gulp. She poured herself another shot. "I wish. No, I was born in the forties, when women were meant to be housewives and nothing more. I was bored out of my skull, and I spent most of my adult life depressed as anything. It didn't help that my husband, Joseph, took it badly when we couldn't conceive."

"I'm sorry."

"Don't be. I would have been a terrible mother. I don't mind other people's kids, but that's because you can hand them back after a few minutes. The fact that one of us was infertile was a blessing."

"So you lived like a regular housewife? I honestly can't believe it."

Dot nodded. "Yes. Then one day, I met Rosie, working at the bank. And I saw she had something to her, something more. We went out for coffee, and I made a decision: I had lived my life on other people's terms for forty-five years. I wasn't about to do the same for the next forty-five."

I grinned. "What did you do?"

"I got rid of Joseph, for one."

"Is that you admitting to murder?"

"I wish. No, I simply moved out. I found out later

he was banging his secretary. Everything about our lives was a cliché. He was so mad. He swore as I was packing that if I went through with this, he'd find me and kill me. So I grabbed the biggest knife from the block in the kitchen and told him I had much more experience with it than he did. I don't think he thought I was seriously going to go through with it until then."

"But you did."

"You better believe it. I was forty-five years old, and I felt like I was twenty. I slept on Rosie's couch until I was able to get on my feet. Everything I owned fit in the back of a Corolla, and I'd never been happier in my life. I'm telling you, the minute you leave the expectations of others behind, that's when you truly start *living*."

"So you've been on your own ever since?"

"Sure have. Joseph would get drunk and leave threatening phone calls on my answering machine from time to time, but I wasn't scared of him. He didn't have it in him to come after me. And a few years later, he died anyway. Heart attack, right in the middle of doing the dirty with the secretary he'd been sleeping with. And I never looked back."

"Huh," I said, leaning back in the lounger. "I never would have guessed."

"One thing I've learned: it takes a lot of courage to go after what you want in life. It's not easy. If it was, everyone would be happy. I was scared out of my wits, but I've also never been happier."

"I'm glad you got there in the end."

"Me too. Though I won't lie, I do wish I'd realized it twenty years earlier. Still, being at the school and having access to books was enough for a while. That was where I learned how to use computers and how hacking worked."

"Really? As a school librarian?"

"Of course. I had access to a whole catalogue of books and, with the emergence of technology, plenty of reasons to buy books on computers."

"That's really cool. I'm glad you eventually found yourself."

"So am I, Charlie. So am I."

Chapter 25

About an hour later, Rosie returned, snacks in hand, and Dot got into Queenie while Rosie drove her car behind us to take Dot home once she dropped us off.

I'd had altogether too much scotch and was well and truly sloshed by the time we left Dot's apartment.

"I wish I knew who killed Jo," I slurred as we drove along. "I want them to rot in jail, not just for murdering her but also for trying to frame someone else for having done it. That's bad karma."

"Sure is," Dot replied.

"Can't your computer find out who did it?"

Dot chuckled. "I'm afraid that while it's good, it's not *that* good."

"I bet the NSA has a satellite or something somewhere that's recording everything. They'd probably be able to find the killer if they wanted to."

"It's very possible," Dot replied. "Unfortunately, if that is the case, it's so well encrypted even I can't get in. And it's not the sort of thing I'd want to do on a computer anywhere near home, either. So we're just going to have to find the killer the old-fashioned way."

"Beating people up with baseball bats until they tell us the truth?"

"Using our brains. But we'll start in the morning, when you're in better shape."

"I'm in fine shape now. To use my brain and a baseball bat."

"Yes, if that shape is a slug. You literally look like you're melting into the seat. But right now, I'll consider it a win if you don't puke all over yourself before getting home."

"That is always a win. This is your fault though. I only brought wine. You tempted me with the scotch."

"That I did," Dot chuckled. "But then, I only poured out a couple fingers. You did the rest. Either way, we're here."

"Do I really have to get out of the car?"

"No. But eventually, you're going to have to pee. Also, seeing as someone tried to kill you today, you're probably safer in your apartment."

Dot and Rosie both helped me out of the car as I began the long trudge up to my apartment. Jesper was sitting in a lounge chair outside the front door, tanning herself.

"Been day drinking, huh?" she greeted us. "Don't worry, I won't judge."

"Good, because I've earned this. Someone shot at me today," I said to my neighbor.

"That's a good reason. I was in a bank during an

armed robbery once, in Honolulu. One of the hostages was shot in the arm, but I was wearing a long skirt, so when he wasn't looking, I unclipped my leg. The thief came by, and when he passed, I hit him over the head with it. Knocked him out, and the cops came in. I've never been happier to have a removable leg in my life."

"Well, as great as that story is, I'd like us to get out of here before Charlie pukes all over everything," Dot said. "It's nice to meet you."

"You too," Jesper said, either ignoring or not having noticed the askance look Rosie gave when she told the story. At least one of my friends was very skeptical as to the truth.

Dot and Rosie dropped me off in the house, I was pretty sure I thanked them, and before I knew it, I was passed out.

I WOKE UP IN THE MIDDLE OF THE NIGHT WITH A pounding headache. My desire to stay in bed fought with an intense need to pee, but the latter won out. After all, my bed was going to be far less comfortable if I ignored nature's call.

I imagined Zoe was probably at work or asleep like a normal person at this hour of the night. Checking my phone—how had it gotten plugged in next to the bed? I was going to have to thank Dot and Rosie for taking such good care of me—I groaned when I saw the time: 2:57. It was too early to be awake.

When I got back from the bathroom, I also found a glass of water and a bottle of Advil on the night-stand. Dot and Rosie really *had* taken care of me. I slipped back into bed, closing my eyes to try and get rid of the pounding behind them, but it didn't work.

I got up and went to the living room, where the TV was set up. I turned on the DVR; Zoe had brought the box over from her old apartment, so all of her recordings were still on it. I scanned through what she had, since anything was better than the late-night infomercials that dominated the airwaves at this hour.

"Come on, Zoe. How many Ken Burns documentaries and shows about whales does one person need?" I muttered aloud. "They're big, they eat stuff in the sea, and they go 'OooooOOOOOooooOOOOoo.' There. Saved you an hour."

Somewhere in the hospital a few miles away, I was pretty sure Zoe had just instinctively rolled her eyes and didn't know why. Luckily, after scrolling a bit, I found some old episodes of *The Wire*. I put one on; it was the episode where Cheese Wagstaff was shot in the arm. One of the early seasons.

Method Man did a really good job with that role, I thought to myself halfway through the episode.

And then it hit me.

I knew who had killed Jo Lismore.

I bounded up from the couch and grabbed my phone, texting Dot. I needed an address.

To my surprise, she answered about two minutes later.

Why are you up? I sent back in reply. I hadn't really

been expecting to hear from her for at least a few hours.

I think what you're looking for is 'thank you'.

Oh yeah. Thanks!!

Is he the killer?

I'm pretty sure, yeah.

Are you going to go over there?

I don't know. Maybe I should wait until he goes to work.

That's a good idea.

My heart pounded in my chest as I looked up the address on Google Maps. The killer lived on Aiai Street, right by the airport, in a small bungalow. That had to be it. It made perfect sense.

Adrenaline coursed through me as the whole thing came together, and I paced around the room, the TV forgotten. I had to do something.

I couldn't just wait until morning. I had to find out now.

I grabbed my keys and headed to the parking lot, jumping into Queenie and throwing her into gear. Nothing cleared up a bit of a hangover like the adrenaline that came from identifying a killer. I sped down the near-empty Maui streets until I reached Jonathan's home.

Killing the engine and the lights, I let my eyes adjust as I checked out the home of the man I was sure had killed Jo Lismore and tried to frame Sean Sherman for it.

He lived in a small bungalow, an older building with light paint peeling off the wood siding. The lawn was patchy and bare—landscaping obviously wasn't a priority for him—and a ten-year-old Nissan SUV sat next to the house along a gravel drive.

On the back of the vehicle was a Wu-Tang Clan bumper sticker. It was black, with the yellow W that one of the kids at the restaurant had mistaken for a Batman symbol. I wasn't sure who should be more embarrassed: me for being so old I knew more about the Wu-Tang Clan than a teenage boy, or him for not recognizing the logo of one of the world's biggest rap groups.

No, I did know who should be more embarrassed. It was the kid. One hundred percent. *Really, dude, it's the Wu-Tang Clan.* How did he *not* recognize it?

Well, the important thing was that I did. At least, eventually. And that was when it had all clicked. Jonathan had had a Wu-Tang desktop on his computer. He was obviously a huge fan. He was eating fun-size chocolates when I met him, much like the wrappers at Sean Sherman's house.

Jonathan had seemed like a nice, honest guy who gave me straight answers, but in reality, none of them matched up with what other people said about Jo. Jonathan had said she had wanted to become big, really big. Bigger than Elon Musk. But nobody else seemed to think that was Jo's ambition. The others all saw her as a woman who tried to rebel against her father's attempts at guiding her through life, and the fact that she'd gone into drug dealing backed that up.

So why had Jonathan lied? My bet was he wanted to take over the company himself. He probably imag-ined that with Jo dead, Randall would move to retire and put someone else in charge of his business. After all, with no daughter to take over and so many memories of her working there, why would he continue? I figured he was probably right.

But it was going to be pretty hard to do that from jail.

I needed some evidence that he was the killer. But I also wasn't an idiot. It might have been almost four in the morning, but I wasn't about to run into his house and start ransacking it with him presumably asleep inside. I could wait here until he left for work and then go in, when I wouldn't be caught by a murderer.

I figured I could run through all of the possibilities until then and maybe do a Starbucks run for a bit of energy, but at least the adrenaline combined with the Advil had done good work in ridding me of my headache.

Before I had a chance, however, I spotted movement coming from the house. I ducked low in the driver's seat of the car, even though I was parked a couple houses down from Jonathan's, and there was very little light. I still didn't want to risk him spotting me.

Luckily, he didn't so much as glance down the street before hopping into his Nissan and driving off.

Perfect. I waited about two minutes to make sure he wasn't just driving around the block and coming back then hopped out of the car and jogged over toward his house. If there was any solid evidence in here that he was the killer, I was going to get it.

Chapter 26

I realized as I approached the house that I probably should have worn *something* to disguise my appearance. After all, everybody had a Nest camera these days, and I didn't want to run the risk that Jonathan was one of those people and that he'd look over the tape and find me on it. Therefore, I carefully avoided the front part of the building, crossing the street and passing behind the neighbor's hedge before cutting back across to the rear of Jonathan's house.

Of course, I was running the risk that he had a roommate, but this was a small bungalow; it couldn't have been more than about seven or eight hundred square feet, and there were no other cars in the driveway, both of which made me think he probably lived here alone. But I couldn't be sure without knocking on the front door.

Oh well. If he did have a roommate, hopefully they were a sound sleeper.

I pushed the thought to the back of my head as I

peered through one of the windows at the side of the house. I was looking into an open-plan kitchen, living, and dining room. Unfortunately, it's not like there was some sort of giant sign that read "I killed Jo Lismore" hanging over the couch as if this was the world's worst birthday party. I was going to have to go in and find evidence of the murder.

Yanking on the window, I raised my eyebrows slightly when it easily slid open. That was lucky; Jonathan must have forgotten to lock it at some point. The window was pretty low to the ground, as the older bungalow had relatively low ceilings, but I was still a very weak human being, physically.

I totally had to start going to the gym. I tried hoisting myself up onto the ledge, but my arms wouldn't support my body weight. Eventually, I simply jumped up as high as I could, landed on the ledge with my stomach, and let the momentum carry me head-first into the house, sliding forward like the world's least subtle slug.

I landed in a heap on the living room floor. If Jonathan had a roommate, I was going to find out about it sooner rather than later, because there was no way any human would sleep through that. I paused for a moment, crouched and ready to run in case I was accosted by a roommate with a baseball bat, but instead I was met with silence, the only thing I could hear being the sound of my heart racing a million beats a minute inside my chest.

With every passing second, I began to relax a bit more, and I stood up, looking around the house. That was when I realized I really didn't have a plan here. What was I hoping to find? Evidence that Jonathan had killed Jo, of course. But what evidence could there be? The gun had been found in Sean Sherman's apartment.

Crap.

Maybe I should have thought about this *before* committing a felony.

But hey, it was too late now. Besides, there was always a chance I'd find something good. Maybe the gun that he had used to try and kill me earlier that day. Then again, maybe he'd gone out to get rid of it. Four in the morning would be a good time to drive up the highway and dump the gun in the ocean.

Whatever. I was here now. I didn't have anything better to do than look around and hope I found something that could prove Jonathan was the killer.

I pulled out my phone, turned on the flashlight, and scanned the open space. It certainly looked neater than Sean Sherman's apartment had. Jonathan obviously understood how to use a dishwasher and that leftover food went into the garbage, among other things. The furniture was mostly older but taken care of. It looked like the furniture of a well-adjusted single man in his early thirties, really.

I headed to the bookshelf next to the television and began scanning the titles and running my hand behind the books to see if there was anything hidden back there, anything that might prove Jonathan was the killer.

On the far side was a small desk with a laptop,

where Jonathan kept his bank statements and bills. I had a quick look through them. He made decent money working for Randall's company, but his mortgage was expensive, and he didn't seem to have a lot left over at the end of the day. In fact, his credit card balances betrayed the fact that he lived beyond his means.

No wonder he wanted to take over the company. Beneath all the bills was a typed out letter, and as soon as I saw it, I knew I had the motive nailed down.

It was written to Randall and dated a month from now. Obviously, Jonathan had been working hard at it and was hanging onto it for some time. There were plenty of crossed-out words and changed items.

Randall,

Given the situation with Jo's tragic death and the painful memories you must have every time you step into the building, I have a proposition to make for you.

I would like to purchase the company from you at a fair price and organize an in-house payment plan in which you would finance the purchase and I would repay you over the course of a specified period of time.

We can discuss details such as you staying on as a partial investor, perhaps more hands-off if you'd like to stay away from the business, but I would like to speak with you about this further if this is an idea that interests you.

The company has been my home for the last few years, and I strongly believe I can take it to the next level. I had always planned on doing so alongside Jo, but with that no longer being an option, I would like to try doing so on my own, giving you the option of stepping away if that's what you desire.

Please let me know your thoughts. You know where to find me.

Jonathan

Right. I'd nailed the motive head-on. He wanted Jo out of the way so he could buy the company. He needed the in-house financing because given what I'd just seen on his bank statements, there was no way any legitimate financial corporation would give him a loan of the size he needed.

I tucked the letter into my pants pocket. I was sure Jake would find it really interesting, especially if it was just slid under his door and he couldn't prove it came from me.

"Well, well, well. If it isn't Randall's pesky little private investigator."

I froze in place as Jonathan's voice reverberated across the room. I was caught. I turned to face him.

He had a gun pointed at me; a gun that looked suspiciously like the kind James Bond used. This was probably the same weapon he'd used to try to kill me the previous afternoon.

"I thought you'd gone out," I said slowly, trying to keep calm. It was really, really hard not to panic when a gun was pointed at my chest.

"That was what I wanted you to think. I saw you parked out there, checking out this place, and I knew you'd figured me out."

"Yeah. You killed Jo, and you tried to kill me yesterday too."

"You keep coming back to the business. I knew you were going to be onto me eventually. I had to get rid of you before you did. And now I've got my shot."

"If you kill me here, it's going to be a lot harder to hide," I pointed out quickly. "And sure, you could always claim self-defense and that I broke in here, and you'd probably even get away with it, but that would then bring on more questions about Jo's death. If they weren't already, they'd start looking at you for it. So you have to ask yourself if you really want to shoot me in the middle of your living room, or if that's going to cause even more trouble for you."

Jonathan's eyes narrowed, and the gun twitched in his hand. "I'm certainly not going to let you go."

"No, I wouldn't expect you to at this point. But doing this here isn't smart. You're going to get caught."

I was just trying to buy myself more time. "Why don't you start telling me why you framed Sean for the murder? You planted the gun at his house."

Jonathan laughed, an empty, hollow sound with no humor behind it. "He was the perfect fall guy. I knew for months I was going to kill Jo. I was her boss! I was better than her at business. She was just a drug dealer who vaguely knew how to code and had zero interest in the company, and yet *she* was supposed to take it over? Why? Because she was born into the right family? It just wasn't fair. I knew if she was out of the picture that not only would I be in a prime position to take over, but if she was dead, her father would want to get rid of the company entirely. So I planned it all out. Sean had been missing work or coming to work stoned for a couple of months. I knew he was going to have to go, but instead of doing it myself as I normally would, I got Jo to do it under the guise of giving her additional business experience."

"And instead, you gave Sean a great motive to kill her."

Jonathan grinned. "It was kind of genius if you think about it."

"You knew about the drug dealing, then?"

Jonathan snorted. "Everyone at the office knew about the drug dealing. Well, everyone except her father, anyway. If he suspected, he managed to look the other way, at any rate. I think he knew she wasn't the perfect daughter he had always wanted, but he desperately needed to believe she would take over his business one day. Well, she didn't."

"So, one day, after Jo died, you went to Sean's apartment. Let me guess, under the guise of making a friendly offer for a reference or something like that?"

"Exactly right. I told him there were no hard feelings, that if he ever needed a reference for a job that he was welcome to put me down, all that crap. Sean was so high he was barely functioning, and when he went to the bathroom, I slipped the gun behind his couch. He didn't have a clue. It was the easiest part of the whole thing."

"The only problem was you left a couple wrappers from that candy you were always eating on the table near the drugs. I should have picked up on it earlier."

"Oh, well. I'm sure they're long gone now. Besides, it's not like I'm the only person in the world who eats bite-sized candy all year. Well, now you can go to your grave knowing the whole story."

"All right," I said, gulping hard as I realized it was basically now or never. "Where are you going to kill me?"

"I'm not sure yet. Why don't we go for a drive? You take the keys. They're right here." He held them up and jingled them.

"Sure. Toss them over. I don't want to get too close to that gun. You understand."

Jonathan paused as if considering whether that was a good idea. Then he gave me a curt nod and threw them my way.

Male privilege was about to work out super well for me. Jonathan had obviously never walked down a dark street at night with his car keys between his fingers in case he was attacked or even considered that it was a thing someone could do.

"Okay, I'm coming," I said. I walked toward him, trying to keep him from noticing as I pressed the keys into my palm and carefully jammed the car one between two of my fingers. I was going to have one try at this, and there was a good chance I'd be shot.

But I mean, at this point, I knew he was going to shoot me anyway, so I could risk getting shot trying to escape, or I could just go to my death without fighting back.

Obviously the first one was the better idea.

"Come on," he said, glancing at his clock. "I need you to die before anyone gets up."

"I'm coming," I said, picking up the pace.

Jonathan kept the gun trained on me, and as I reached him, I used the oldest trick in the book: I carefully slipped my own car keys from my pocket and threw them behind me.

At the sound of clacking, Jonathan instinctively turned around, the gun moving just away from me. I took the opportunity. I drove his own car key as hard as I could into his neck.

He screamed, shooting the gun, and I jumped. There was no pain, so I was pretty sure I wasn't hurt. I wasn't going to sit around and wait to find out what I'd done to him. I let go of the key and ran, picking my keys back up and sprinting toward the front door. If I could just get back to Queenie without being shot, I'd be fine.

"Get back here, you bitch!" Jonathan roared, footsteps pounding after me. Then there came a thudding sound, and the footsteps stopped.

"Charlie," a familiar voice called out.

I stopped to see Dot waving at me, while Rosie kicked the gun away from Jonathan's hand. He was lying on the ground on the doorstep, bleeding pretty badly from his neck. His hands clutched at his face, while a baseball bat lay on the ground next to him.

"I think you may have nicked his jugular," Rosie said, taking off her sweater.

Jonathan screamed as he writhed on the ground. "Leave me alone!"

"If I leave you, you're going to die, and believe me, it's not fun watching a man slowly bleed to death," Rosie told him, calm as anything. "Dot, would you mind calling an ambulance?"

"I mean, do we have to?" Dot asked.

Rosie shot her a look. "Yes. Not for him, but for Jo's family."

"Fine," Dot huffed, pulling out her phone as Rosie wrapped the sweater around Jonathan's neck.

"I can't breathe," he shouted.

"If you couldn't breathe, you wouldn't be able to yell that. Now, be quiet. I'm saving your life, which is more than you deserve, and it won't take much to convince me to let you die here."

That certainly shut Jonathan up, and his cries turned into more of a whimper.

I pulled out my phone and called Jake.

"Yes?" he answered, his voice thick with sleep.

"It's Charlie."

"Is anyone dead?"

"Almost," I replied. "It took a bit of convincing, but Dot's calling an ambulance now."

"Who is it?"

"Jonathan Keegan, Jo's boss and murderer. He wanted to take over the business. Oh, and he's also the one who tried to shoot me yesterday. But I can tell you that story later."

"Where are you?" Jake asked, and the shuffling noise in the background told me he was getting dressed.

"Jonathan's house. Aiai Street, by the airport."

"I know it. I'll be there soon."

I hung up the phone and watched as Rosie did her

best to keep Jonathan calm while we waited for the ambulance.

A few minutes later, the sound of sirens began piercing the air, getting progressively louder. It looked as if Jonathan was going to make it.

Chapter 27

The EMTs were just getting ready to load Jonathan onto the stretcher when Jake arrived, pulling up to the crime scene in a flashy red Tesla Model S. He screeched to a stop and stepped out of the car, immediately making his way to the scene.

"Are you all right?" he asked, and I nodded.

"I'm fine."

"Arrest her and her old friends," Jonathan shouted from the stretcher. "They tried to kill me."

"In my defense, he tried to kill me first," I offered up with a shrug. "Also, he admitted to me that he killed Jo."

"What were you even doing here?"

"Looking for evidence he killed Jo."

"Legally?" Jake's eyes narrowed.

"Totally. You know me; I'd never break the law."

"Right. Let me call this in; I'll have a unit meet the ambulance at the hospital and arrest him." Jake pulled out his phone and jumped into the ambulance.

A moment later, Jonathan's voice called out. "What the hell? Why are you arresting me? I'm the victim here!"

I laughed and headed over to Dot and Rosie. "Why were you guys here, anyway?"

"When you texted me that you thought he was the killer, I thought I'd scope him out just in case he tried to make a run for it," Dot said. "Obviously, Rosie wanted to come along."

"It's been so many years since I've gotten a phone call in the middle of the night to get involved in an investigation," Rosie said, her face lighting up. "I'd forgotten how good it feels. The adrenaline rush, the long hours of a stakeout. Of course, in this case, it wasn't that many hours."

"He left because he saw me coming."

"Charlie, I love you like a daughter, and you have some great traits, but subtlety is not one of them," Rosie said kindly. "If you'd like to learn how to truly spy on someone in the middle of the night, I can teach you, because driving up to someone's home in a Jeep that sounds like Air Force One taking off, painted in a color that would make Lady Gaga blush, is not it."

"Wait, you were here the whole time I was? I had no idea. I never saw you."

"Exactly," Rosie said, looking satisfied. "As soon as we saw Jonathan return, we knew he was going to harm you. We figured he wouldn't do it inside the home, as it would be too hard to explain away, so we waited for him to come out. What did you do to him?"

"Stabbed him in the neck with his own car keys," I

said, looking down. It was only then that I realized my hands were covered in Jonathan's blood. Ew.

"Good thinking," Rosie said. "I assume you were trying to run back to your car?"

"Exactly. My main goal was getting away. It helped that you two were there. Where did the baseball bat come from?"

"After the last few days, I figured it was probably a good idea to keep it in the trunk just in case," Dot said. "But if anyone asks, we found it on the lawn."

I nodded. "Good call."

Jake came out from the ambulance then and headed toward us. "I didn't get nearly enough sleep for this," he said. "But I'm going to have to take statements from all of you."

Twenty minutes later, Jake announced we were free to go. "And please, for the love of all that is holy, try not to commit any more crimes for the rest of the day."

"That's a weird way of saying 'thank you for finding a murderer for me,' but okay," I replied.

"Yes. I do have to admit, I wasn't looking at Jonathan at all. So thank you. Jo will be getting justice thanks to you." He even offered me a small smile that lit up his face.

I wanted to lean over and kiss those lips and immediately forced the thought from my mind. Wow. It had been *way* too long since I'd gotten laid if I was willing to give it up for Jake. I mean, sure, he was insanely hot, in an annoying kind of way, but I had standards.

Or so I told myself.

"All in a day's work," I replied.

"Speaking of, it's time for you to retire back to serving ice cream. That's far less dangerous for everyone involved."

"Fine with me. I never really intended to do this as a job, anyway. Randall came to me."

"Yes. Well, if you get another opportunity of the sort, please don't take it. You almost died *again*. And I really, really don't want to come across a crime scene where you're the victim." The sincerity in his words was obvious.

"I'll do my best not to get murdered," I replied.

"And you two," he said, looking toward Dot and Rosie, who gave him their sweetest, most grandmotherly looks, which I knew were just ruses. "I don't know what you were thinking, or why you were here with Charlie, but you're certainly old enough to know better than to be involving yourselves in this sort of thing."

"Young man, you have no business telling us what we can and can't do," Dot said, crossing her arms in front of her.

Jake looked taken aback for a split second but recovered quickly. "I'm the police. That's exactly what my business is."

"So long as we're not breaking the law, we can do what we want. Just because we're old doesn't mean we're useless."

"That's not at all what I... you know what, never mind. Just stay out of trouble. Please. I really hope I don't see you around." He turned and left, muttering, "I don't get paid enough for this," under his breath as he walked back to his car.

A smile flittered on my lips as I turned to Dot and Rosie. "All right, well, I have a few hours to go before my shift at Aloha Ice Cream starts. Who wants to get breakfast while I down a liter of espresso shots to get through the day?"

"That sounds great. And it's after four in the morning, so we're just in time for the senior deal at my favorite diner, though we'll have to get going quickly, as rush hour will be starting soon," Dot said.

I laughed and shook my head as I followed my friends back to their car.

"I HAVE TO SAY, I DO WORRY ABOUT PHIL McCracken," I said as I poured copious amounts of ketchup onto the hash browns and fried eggs that had appeared in front of me, careful not to let any of it touch the coconut French toast with passionfruit topping next to it. "I mean, I assume the guys he owes that cash Jo stiffed him are bad dudes."

"You don't have to worry about him," Rosie said. "We took care of it."

I raised an eyebrow. "Took care of it how?"

"He's not dead if that's what you're thinking," Dot replied.

That's exactly what I was thinking.

"We made a trade. Rosie reached out to some old

contacts and got him a new identity, a plane ride to the mainland, enough cash to get him through for a few months, and a promise that he'd be staying out of the drug-dealing business for good. I'm pretty sure he'll keep that promise; she scared him pretty good."

"I told him I'd be watching him, and I know he believed me," Rosie said proudly. "In exchange, he gave us enough evidence on his bosses that will get them locked up for good, when it's all anonymously delivered to the police. We really had no evidence on him at all, and this way hopefully with his suppliers getting locked up it'll limit the supply of fentanyl being brought onto the island."

I chuckled as I took a bite of my food. "Well, I'm glad it's worked out, then. What name did you give him? Surely there's nothing worse than Phil McCracken."

"Mike Litoris," Rosie replied with a grin.

I choked on the piece of egg I was chewing. "No way."

"Hey, he's certainly not completely innocent of any crimes. He deserved a little bit of karma coming his way. Besides, he can always go by Michael."

"I'm… not sure that's much better. I'm going to have to see Randall this morning as well. At least this time, I can give him a definite answer."

"Yes. It will hurt, but hopefully, over the long term, having that closure will help the family heal," Rosie said. "Still, they'll be going through it for a long time."

"I imagine Randall will have a hell of a time trying to forgive himself for hiring Jonathan," Dot said. "Even though he couldn't have known he was going to end up with a psychopathic employee who killed his daughter so he could buy the company."

"No kidding," I replied, digging into the coconut French toast. "Well, I have to say, as much as this was interesting, and I'm even more financially set than before, I'll be glad to get back to the ice cream shop, where drunk idiots trying to rob me and horny guys flirting are the worst things I have to deal with."

Rosie gave me a knowing smile. "You say that now, but I see the adventure that lives inside of you. Should you change your mind, do let us know. I've been rather enjoying our adventures."

"By the way, I looked up that fantastical story your neighbor told us about beating a robber with her prosthetic," Dot said. "I was sure it was going to be total bunk."

"Oh, yeah, Leslie knows Jesper and said she has a propensity to exaggerate a little when it comes to stories about her leg."

"As it turns out, in this case, it's one hundred percent real."

"Wait, really?" I asked.

Dot nodded enthusiastically. "Oh, yes. It happened a few years ago. She clubbed the robber with her fake leg, and he was caught. She even got an award from the governor for it."

"That must have been when we went on that safari in Africa," Rosie said to Dot. "We would have missed all of it."

"Of course. We were gone for two months; there's

no way I'd have missed news like that while we were in town. You'll have to introduce us formally. Your new neighbor sounds fun."

I laughed. "Will do. I'm sure Jesper will love the two of you too."

That was just what this island needed: my two crazy old friends getting together with my even crazier neighbor. Things would never be the same.

As I sat in a diner at five in the morning, single-handedly bringing the average age of the clientele down by decades, I took another bite of the coconut French toast and smiled. I was alive, the sun would be shining in a few hours, and it was yet another beautiful day in paradise.

It felt as if nothing in the world could go wrong.

BOOK 3 - BEACHSIDE BULLET: CHARLIE IS TAKING the plunge to become a private investigator, and her first official case is a doozy. When three of Zoe's coworkers are shot in a brazen mid-day attack, Charlie is initially content to let the police deal with it. But when it becomes obvious the detective in charge has the IQ of a box of crayons, she decides to step in to ensure the killer is found.

What appears at first glance to be a random attack quickly becomes more than that, and before she knows it Charlie finds herself scouring the island for a murderer, with the help of Dot and Rosie, of course.

In case hunting down a shooter wasn't enough,

Charlie quickly nets herself another customer in the form of her eight-year-old neighbor. And of course, Charlie isn't expecting Jake to take the news of her new career very well. Luckily, Charlie isn't especially worried about his opinion, especially when she has so much on her plate.

Is Charlie about to make a splash in her new career, or will she quickly find herself drowning, instead?

Click here to pre-order Beachside Bullet now (coming November 2021)

About the Author

Jasmine Webb is a thirty-something who lives in the mountains most of the year, dreaming of the beach. When she's not writing stories you can find her chasing her old dog around, hiking up moderately-sized hills, or playing Pokemon Go.

Sign up for Jasmine's newsletter to be the first to find out about new releases here: http://www.authorjasminewebb.com/newsletter

You can also join Jasmine's Facebook Reader group here:
http://www.facebook.com/groups/jasminewebb

You can also connect with her on other social media here:

A Note from the Author

Hi! I just wanted to say thank you for reading Maui Murder. I really hope you enjoyed this book, because I had a blast writing it.

If you'd like to help other readers find this book as well, please consider leaving a review on Amazon or Goodreads, or on whatever platform you purchased this book.

I have plenty of stories for Charlie and friends coming up in the future, and you can preorder Beachside Bullet, the third book in the series, now. The planned release is for the end of November, but if I'm finished before then I might release it early.

Until next time, I hope you're able to enjoy some sunshine, and that every book you read brings you unhinged joy.

Jasmine

Also by Jasmine Webb

Charlotte Gibson Mysteries

Aloha Alibi

Maui Murder

Beachside Bullet (Coming November 2020)